one hundred words

ALSO BY LAUREN HALLSTROM

Dreamweaver

one hundred words

Lauren Hallstrom

To Rebecca –
Friendship is forever.

Prologue

There is magic in words.

Ink spirals across the page, forming curves, then letters and, finally, words. The words begin to take shape, and soon they will transform into something else entirely.

A story.

The words, scrawled across the page in hurried script, hold a certain raw beauty that only comes from such honesty and simplicity. They seem to have minds of their own as they race on, almost out of control.

Soon, the page is filled and the ink, dark as night, still flows, the lifeblood of the story that courses through the pages and reverberates with pure power.

My hands are stained with ink—ink that I know will never come off—but I don't care. The story is ingrained in my mind, and now the memory of it will never fade. Ink runs through my veins until I am not so different from what I am writing. I am the story, and it is me.

This is what I feel when I write. If the words come out just right, they can create something that is beautiful, powerful, and inescapable. In this way, words have shaped every moment of my life. They have haunted me and turned me into who I am now.

And then it happened… I wrote one story that was different from the rest. I never expected my words to have the power to not only bring a story to life, but also to condemn a person to death.

Now I am caught between fiction and reality, past and present, and it's only a matter of time before they collide.

Chapter One

I slammed my fists down on the keyboard in front of me, making lines of gibberish stream across the blank page of the document on my computer screen. Groaning aloud in frustration, I angrily jabbed at the backspace button to make it all go away.

Above all, the one thing I couldn't stand was writer's block. For someone who had been writing nearly all her life, you'd have thought it would no longer be a problem. But lately, all the words just seemed to escape me.

Hoping I could somehow gain inspiration by staring at the blank screen, I returned my gaze to my computer, but to no avail. I stifled another groan. How could I call myself a writer if I couldn't write?

With sudden firm resolve, I placed my fingers on

the keyboard, ready to type something—anything. It didn't matter anymore as long as I got something down on the page.

"Tess!" The sudden, loud voice coming from downstairs made me jump, and I almost knocked over the cup of tea sitting next to my computer on the desk. I sighed, slapping the laptop shut. At this rate, I would never get anything done.

"Yes, Mom?" I called out just loud enough to be heard through the closed door of my bedroom. This was how our conversations went these days—yelling across the house, or even face to face. I didn't like the prospect of leaving my room when all I had gained from staring at the screen was a blank page, but it couldn't be helped. My mother would give me no peace until I did.

"Come downstairs and eat with us, please. I've held dinner for over an hour already."

At her words, I felt a little guilty that I had wasted so much of her time—and mine—staring at a blank computer page. Mom disliked cooking, and she usually had just enough energy to buy takeout meals on the way home from the preschool where she taught. With a classroom of energetic four-year-olds to care for on weekdays, Mom had her hands full. Since today was Friday, she had stayed late at the school with the other preschool teacher, Ms. Wilson, to plan for next week. Today happened to be the one night in months that she was able to summon up the will to make us a real home-cooked dinner, and here I was holed up in my room trying to find the perfect words while dinner grew cold.

I got up from my chair, nearly overturning it in my haste. It had already started to grow dark out, and the light in my room had dimmed. My long wooden desk cast strange, angular shadows against the walls, and my shelves of carefully arranged encyclopedias and other reference books were mounted on the wall above the desk. My bed at the opposite corner of the room was neatly made, and the surfaces of my dresser and nightstand were clear. Around my desk, though, papers and books were strewn across the floor. Not bothering to take the time to pick them up, I hurried from the room.

When I entered the kitchen, Mom was sitting at the table alone, her hands clasped together in her lap. Her shoulders were slumped and her usually neat, dark brown curls were disheveled.

She looked so small at that moment when she thought no one was watching, so vulnerable. So *alone*. A lump formed in my throat, and I swallowed hard. How could I be so self-centered? I had been so wrapped up in my own troubles with my writing that I had failed to notice that Mom was having a hard time too. It couldn't be easy for her, living with two people who were always off in their own little worlds.

My eyes flicked over to the kitchen table. It was set for three, but two chairs still remained unoccupied. As I hurried over, Mom heaved a heavy, shuddering sigh, but when she noticed I was there she straightened and mustered up a weak smile. I slipped into my seat across from Mom. "Where's Dad?"

Mom looked up at the ceiling. "Where else?"

She meant he was in his studio, which was directly above the kitchen. Dad was up there nearly all the time, immersed in his art much as I was with my writing. He painted constantly; what he painted, though, I had no idea. I was a young girl the last time he'd shown me his work. All I could remember were splashes of blurred color, maybe a landscape. He was good—I knew that much—but Dad never allowed anyone to view his artwork anymore. As far as I knew, it had been years since Mom had seen any of it, either.

A loud bang from upstairs made me jump, and I heard the sound of hurried footsteps on the stairs. A moment later, Dad appeared at the doorway to the kitchen. "Sorry I'm late, guys." He looked in our direction, but his eyes didn't quite focus on us. The vacant expression on his face suggested he was still thinking about his artwork. Mom often told me it was the same expression I wore when I was daydreaming about my writing.

Dad joined us at the table, and although he immediately helped himself to several heaping spoonfuls from the pot in the middle of the table, he hadn't quite managed to shake the absentminded look from his face. I turned to Mom, who was staring daggers at Dad, and I looked away quickly, developing a sudden interest in the glob of Hamburger Helper that Dad had spooned onto my plate.

Mom and Dad were complete opposites. It was a wonder there was ever a time when they weren't fighting. Mom was tidy and was never late for anything in her life, which was why the time Dad spent in his studio bothered her so much. I glanced at Dad, who had paused from eating to sketch something on his napkin with his special sketching pencil that he always had with him. I noticed the dried paint stuck underneath his fingernails and a red streak smeared through his blond, scraggly hair. Whenever he painted, this was how he looked, and I had become accustomed to seeing a small blotch of paint on his skin somewhere. Without it, he wouldn't be the Dad I knew.

I shoved a forkful of Hamburger Helper into my mouth, gagging at the taste. I swallowed with effort, the too-large bite scraping my throat on the way down. The edges of the pasta were hard, and the texture was strange. I didn't know how anyone could mess up a meal as simple as Hamburger Helper, but I supposed it was the thought that counted.

The tense silence was stifling. After a brief period of attempting to interpret my parents' expressions, I let my thoughts turn to my writing. I knew what I wanted to say, but every time I put pen to paper, the words didn't come out right. It was frustrating. Would I ever be able to write the way I wanted to? I longed for the words to naturally transform themselves into prose. For if the words I wrote weren't special, the story wouldn't be either.

Without warning, Mom suddenly set her fork down on her plate and turned to Dad. "Chris, I wish you wouldn't spend so much time in that studio of yours."

It took him a minute to register what she had said. "Huh? What do you mean? It's what I love, you know that."

Mom's eyes hardened. Uh-oh. I stared down at my plate, swirling my fork around in the sauce to create a strange kind of artwork. Silently I willed them to stop. *Please, not now. We all have enough on our minds.*

Evidently Mom didn't hear my unvoiced prayer. "You think this is easy for me?" she cried, staring at Dad. He raised his eyebrows but didn't comment. "I spend all day teaching, and yes, I happen to love doing it, but I don't think you realize how much work I put into it. I have to support all of us, working full-time, five days a week, just so you can have the time to lounge around all day at home, creating your fantasies in paintings that you later just throw away!"

Whoa. Mom's outburst made my stomach churn. Never before had she come right out and said exactly what she thought about Dad's work, though I had guessed she thought as much. "May I be excused?" I couldn't bring myself to lift my eyes from my plate.

Mom whipped her head around to face me. "You certainly may not be excused! I worked hard slaving over the stove for this nice family meal, and we are going to eat it together. No one is going to leave this table until we have finished — and I mean completely finished — this meal. I don't want to see a speck of food on those plates!"

I flinched at her harsh words and glanced over at Dad, who gave me a reassuring smile but didn't say anything in opposition. He must have learned that from years of fighting with her. If he didn't say anything, she couldn't keep arguing forever, I supposed. But I still wished she wouldn't do this.

Tentatively, I pushed the last few forkfuls of Hamburger Helper into my mouth and swallowed with difficulty. "It was a very good dinner, Mom," I offered.

"Hmm," was all she said, but I thought I noticed the corner of her mouth turn up slightly at my compliment. Dad finished at the same time I did, and the three of us stood. Dad carried our dishes to the sink and wordlessly started washing them. It was just to make Mom happy, of course. I knew what his mind was really on now, and I knew where he would go as soon as he was finished.

I headed to the coat rack in the corner of the hallway between the kitchen and the entryway and pulled on my old, worn denim jacket. I could use some fresh air. And maybe a change of setting would give me inspiration for my writing.

"Oh, Tess," Mom sighed, watching me from the other room. "You're not going out tonight, are you? It's already almost dark." She seemed to have calmed down somewhat. At least her face was no longer red, and her pupils weren't quite as dilated as they had been before.

"I know, Mom. It'll only be a little while. I just have…something I need to do."

Mom pressed her lips together tightly, and she looked as if she were about to force me to stay here. "All right," she said finally. "But be back in an hour and no later."

I turned to leave, but just before I closed the front door I heard her muttering to herself. "It's a waste of time. She's never going to be satisfied with her writing, just like Chris is never satisfied with his art. Why can't she be more like me?"

Chapter Two

The playground was obscured by shadows that shrouded the area in darkness, yet kids were still at play. I often made the half-hour walk to this park in the city. Although it was rather far to travel to so frequently, I found myself coming back here again and again, if only because it was a great spot to think. If there was one place that could inspire me to write, this park was it.

I settled onto the stone steps near the playground, pulling out the blue leather-bound notebook I'd left in my jacket pocket since the last time I had come here. Opening it to a fresh page, I smoothed my writing journal so it would lie flat on my lap. Maybe writing on paper would be easier than typing on a keyboard.

As I thought, I rubbed at the birthmark on my

forearm. It was shaped like a half-moon and had been there as long as I could remember, never ceasing to annoy me.

The wind ruffled my hair and I closed my eyes, drinking in the sensation. The park was filled with noise, and I was struck by the steady flow of people who passed by, even at this time of day. But I wouldn't have it any other way.

I watched a young mother on a bench near me rock her baby back and forth in her arms, trying to quiet the baby's piercing cries. On a bright yellow slide, a boy with unruly hair dared his companion to climb it backward. Voices filled the park, but I was in my own little world. When I was alone in a crowd, I was at home.

I took my black ballpoint pen from my pocket and held it in my hand for a moment, motionless. This was the moment I wanted to capture. Oh, if only I could put my thoughts into words. What do you do when you know exactly what you want to write but don't know how to say it?

I breathed in the moment, relaxing slowly now that I was alone. So totally, wonderfully alone. Uninterrupted. Nothing expected of me. I held the pen, hovering over the empty page. One thought came to my mind at that moment, the urgency of it causing me to write a single word.

Bliss

It was how I felt and what I looked for when I wrote. This was a word that was important to me, a word I didn't want to forget.

Ever since I was little, I had collected words, almost like one might collect stamps or coins. My unusual hobby began when I was in kindergarten, forming words with the letters in alphabet soup. That was the day I first began to realize the importance—and danger—of words.

While many of my classmates simply spelled their names, and Sharon, the know-it-all, spelled "school" (but left off the letter "h"), I chose something a little different.

Desolation

I didn't understand why I had chosen that particular word or where I had heard it, but my parents had been fighting a lot at the time. The kindergarten teacher had been shocked and immediately called my parents, making a big fuss about it.

Desolation became the first word that defined me. From then on, I began to look for words everywhere. In books, in conversation, in graffiti on a cement wall in the city. These things that had been dead before—words—came alive with my realization of their meaning. Ever since that first word, *desolation*, I began to assemble a list in the back of my journal that continued to grow with words that inspired me, intrigued me, or just made me *feel* something. My understanding of language escalated, but my fascination with it never ceased. These words meant more to me than anything else in the world.

I flipped to the back of my writing journal and rewrote *bliss* beneath the list of other words I had added over the years. Rifling through the pages, I then returned to the one I had been writing on most recently. Now that I had a truly meaningful word, I looked around me with new eyes. It was only a single word, but now I had *something*, where before I'd had nothing. The page was no longer blank.

I watched as a man in a dark overcoat passed in front of me, a growing sphere of bubble gum protruding from his mouth. It popped suddenly and collapsed in a mess on his face, and he laughed, oblivious to anyone who was watching.

A woman with purple cat-eye glasses and a leopard print coat hurried past, talking on her cell phone so rapidly her words were jumbled and impossible to distinguish. A little boy trailed behind her, studying a pebble in his hand.

A group of three kids slid down the handrail beside me, giggling hysterically and calling out to each other. The last one jumped off the metal bar too early, nearly falling on top of me. "Sorry!" he called over his shoulder as he ran after his friends, unable to wipe the elated grin from his face.

Without realizing it, I had begun to twirl the pen in my hand, flicking it back and forth in thought. I absorbed my surroundings, taking in the events of the day and mulling over each thought one by one, in no particular order. My thoughts turned into a low buzzing in my mind, until I no longer thought in words, but in emotions.

I had an idea. It was just a speck, just the tiniest hint of an idea, but it was a beginning. I pictured her face in my mind and knew the story would soon follow. I was confident that, this time, the words would come. They hadn't yet, but they would.

They had to.

I tore a sheet of paper from the middle of my journal, feeling satisfaction at the decisive sound of the ripping. Sliding my journal into my jacket pocket, I got to my feet. No other ideas were coming to me, and I wasn't about to wait for them. In the meantime, there was something I needed to do right now.

Painstakingly, I penned a sentence on the scrap of paper in my hand. Sometimes all anyone needed were a few well-chosen words to change a horrible day into the best day. Hesitation came over me like it always did, but as usual, I shook it away.

The park was darker now. The shadows had

lengthened to stretch over most of the sidewalk in spite of the illumination the street lights provided. I scanned the pathways and found an empty bench at the edge of the playground. When I reached it, I stepped out of the shadows and into the light of the streetlamp overhead. Before I could change my mind I bent down, placing the scrap of paper on the seat of the park bench, and retreated to the shadow-filled corner by the stone steps, away from the light.

Patting my coat pockets, I searched for my cell phone to check the time, suddenly aware of how late it must be. I only felt my journal and pen; it seemed I had forgotten my phone yet again. I didn't wear a watch either, so I wasn't sure just how late it was. A light breeze ruffled my hair and raised goose bumps on my arms in spite of the jacket I was wearing. I picked up my pace and started heading in the direction of home, hugging myself tightly as the wind grew colder.

A rustling noise came from behind me and I paused, midstride, to look over my shoulder. A figure stood bending over a bench and looking intently at something on the seat. My scrap of paper, I realized. The figure was the young woman in the leopard print coat, one of the people I'd seen walk by earlier.

She picked up the note, read it, and raised her head to look around the park, now enveloped in shadows. Her eyes passed over me and I saw the wonder in her expression. Even from this distance, I thought I could see tears in her eyes. Her lips moved and now she was staring back at the paper, mouthing the words. I knew exactly what she saw: *You're not in this alone.*

The woman called out to one of the boys still running around the playground and he came up to her, panting. Her son, I guessed. As I watched that moment, I pressed my cheek to the cold concrete of the side of the building I was leaning against near the steps. The woman hugged her son and I blinked back a few stray tears of my own. I straightened then, satisfied that my words had meant something to her, and I turned to leave. Before I had gotten more than a few steps away, though, a glint of gold in the sandbox in the corner of the playground caught my eye, and I started toward it.

When I reached the place where I had seen the flash, I stooped down and pulled the object from the sand. It was a gleaming gold pen. I fingered it, turning it over in my hands.

Despite the fact that the pen had been half-buried in sand, there was not a speck of dirt on it. It seemed brand new. Who would leave behind something as special as this?

Even in the darkness the pen shone brightly. It was one of those elegant fountain pens that had an ink cartridge instead of a refillable reservoir. It was beautiful and unique, yet simple.

It was exactly the kind of pen I had always wanted.

I surveyed the area around me and was surprised to be met with emptiness. A lone owl hooted, making me jump. In the time that I hadn't been looking, the park had cleared, and now I was alone.

Not quite alone. When I glanced around a second time, I spotted the lady in the leopard print coat and her son, still there. The mother was just pulling the strap of her handbag over her shoulder, my note still clutched in her thin fingers. I rushed up to her.

When I reached her, I grew flustered and had to make the greatest effort to look her in the eyes. "Um, excuse me, ma'am. Did you lose this pen?"

She startled and glanced up at me, then down at the pen I held in my outstretched hand. She studied it for a moment, then shook her head. "No, I don't believe I did. Why don't you keep it? It's such a lovely pen. It would be a shame for it to go to waste."

My heart fluttered in relief, but I scolded myself inwardly. I had been half hoping she would say that to give me an excuse to take the pen home with me, even though it was not mine. The saying "finders keepers" popped into my mind, but I brushed it away, feeling silly. "Thank you. Maybe I will."

"You really should." She watched me closely, a peculiar expression on her face that I couldn't quite identify.

I nodded, unable to loosen my grip on the pen, and turned to leave.

"Wait!"

With reluctance, I paused and turned back toward the woman. She looked stricken, but when she saw I had stopped, her eyes softened. "You did this, didn't you?" She held up the scrap of paper I had written on for me to see.

I stared at the ground, glad the darkness concealed the deep flush I could feel creeping across my face. I developed a sudden keen interest in the sidewalk beneath my feet.

"These words," she went on, "They're just beautiful. I know it's hard to believe, but they are exactly what I need to hear. It's just me and my son now, and, well…it's been a little lonely." She turned to look at her son, who grinned back at her. Then her gaze returned to me. "Thank you. I know you did this. You wrote this note, didn't you?"

I was still staring at the ground, but I forced myself to meet her eyes. "Maybe." I couldn't bring myself to say outright that it had been me. What I had done wasn't such a big deal, anyway. I couldn't understand why my words got such strong reactions from the people I gave them to, but I didn't think I deserved their thanks. I was only a messenger, giving the right words to those who seemed to need them.

Before the woman had a chance to speak again, I put my head down and walked quickly away, tucking the golden pen into my pocket before I could convince myself otherwise.

I had barely exited the park before a familiar voice called out to me from behind. "Tess, there you are! I've been looking all over for you."

It was my friend Hazel. I gave her a rare, genuine smile. As I spoke, I let my stiff muscles relax a little. "Hi, Hazel. How's it going?" She was easier for me to talk to than most people.

"You aren't answering your cell phone, girl. Do you even have it on you?"

I shot her a look that said, *I think we both know the answer to that question.*

"Figures," Hazel said, but she grinned back at me. She rocked back and forth on her heels, unable to stay motionless for more than a few moments. Her bright red corkscrew curls bounced up and down as she moved. Hazel was the only person I had known long enough to really call my friend. Those I met on the street or in the park, like the woman in the leopard print coat, were friendly and usually tried to talk to me after I helped them, but they were only acquaintances — people I would likely never see again.

I had known Hazel for about two years now, ever since the beginning of high school. She was a year older than I was, but she was nice enough to stick with me. We were often together, yet I felt like she didn't really understand the real me—the writer who couldn't help but fall in love with every word she heard. Hazel was talkative and bubbly, always trying to convince me to try something new, but it didn't seem like she understood how seriously I took my writing. I was made of words—that was who I was.

Not many people understood my passion for words. They thought I was a pensive, detached loner—someone who shouldn't be bothered with.

Other than Hazel, I had only met one person who thought differently.

I was in third grade, and I had just turned eight. Even then I was often off by myself, reading the same books over and over again until I had each and every word memorized and I could recite the stories from memory. My teacher that year, Ms. Malone, was also unusual. She wore brightly patterned dresses and taught us songs to remember our times tables, rather than using rote memorization.

On Teacher Appreciation Day, I handed Ms. Malone a present I had made especially for her the week before. Nearly a dozen cards were already lined up on her desk in front of her, and she had a new pile of shiny red apples. I remembered wondering if my gift was all wrong.

My teacher paused for what felt like forever while her eyes went back and forth, skimming the page I had handed her. It read:

> *You teach so we will know*
> *Our knowledge will grow,*
> *You show how much you care*
> *By spreading love everywhere.*

Finally, Ms. Malone looked up at me over her thin eyeglasses. "You wrote this poem for me, Tess?"

I nodded hesitantly, thinking back to my kindergarten teacher's reaction to the word *desolation*, spelled out in alphabet soup noodles.

"It's wonderful!" she exclaimed, and I was taken aback. It was such a simple poem.

"You mean you really like it?" I was hopeful.

"I most certainly do!" My teacher gave me a hug, which felt so warm. I couldn't remember the last time my mom had hugged me. "Tess," Ms. Malone said as she regarded me solemnly. She leaned in close. "Don't tell anyone I said this, but I think words are the best gift anyone can give."

∼

I tried to savor the memory, but Hazel jarred me from my reverie. "Earth to Tess! Did you even hear a single word I said?"

I squeezed my eyes shut and then opened them again, ever so slowly. I was still thinking about that sentence: "Words are the best gift." It was something I had never forgotten. After that day, I began giving words away to strangers too. Ms. Malone's words had inspired me, and I strived to do the same for others.

Without warning, a word popped into my head, and I stopped to pull out my notebook and pen and write it on the last page.

Inspire

Meanwhile, Hazel didn't bat an eye. By now she was quite used to my unusual behavior.

One of the words on my list caught my eye.

Malone

I had chosen it after that day in third grade, not only because I admired my teacher but also simply because I thought it was a pretty last name. Once I had finished adding to my growing list, I returned my journal and pen to my pocket, and my thoughts began to wander yet again.

"Come on, Tess. Don't go all glassy-eyed on me again." Hazel's voice broke through my thoughts once more.

I sighed, blinking rapidly a few times in a row.

Hazel was right, I discovered. I forced my eyes to focus on the girl in front of me. "I'm sorry, Hazel. I've just been a little preoccupied lately. The story I've been trying to write isn't working out, and —"

Hazel cut me off, not paying any attention to what I'd just said, which was typical of her. "Oh, don't I know it! I know what you need to loosen yourself up. Some chill time!" She gestured dramatically, waving her hands through the air, which caused the many rings stacked on her fingers to gleam under the streetlight.

"Hazel—" I started, but didn't get any farther.

"No, listen. You need to get out more. There are so many cool things in the world that you're missing out on while you sit holed up in your room by yourself all day." Hazel looked at me pointedly. "I have a great idea! Let's meet at the coffee shop by my house tomorrow and you can meet some of my friends. No big deal, it's just a few other people, and it'll be good for you!" She nudged me, and I had to laugh. "Then we can go to the theater and go see whatever's playing now for like the fifth time. At least, it'll be my fifth time, no matter which movie we pick. As for *you*, I don't remember the last time you set foot in a movie theater."

I shook my head. "I don't know, Hazel, you know how busy I am…" I trailed off, hoping I wouldn't have to say more. Unfortunately, that was not the case.

"Busy staring off into space? Yeah, that takes a lot of energy." When she saw the look on my face, she softened. "Hey, I'm sorry. You know I'm just trying to help, right?"

I sighed. "Yes, I know." Hazel could be pushy and insensitive at times, but she never acted that way on purpose. "All right, I'll go." Just as Hazel started to shout an exclamation of ecstasy, I cut in. "But if you bring more than two people along with you, I'll just curl up in my seat and cower there with my ears covered so I don't have to hear the latest gossip on Justin Bieber."

Hazel shot me a look of mock surprise. "Did I just hear Tess Winters make a joke? What is going on here? Honestly, what is this world coming to?"

Friend

I cracked an unintentional smile and felt myself relax minimally. That was another simple word that was important to me.

"I'd better be getting home," I told Hazel. "Mom will be worried sick."

"Because you never carry your cell phone," Hazel admonished, *tsk-tsk*ing me with her finger.

"So, what are you doing out here at this time of night?"

"Looking for you, of course!" Hazel grinned at me, but something about her expression seemed strange, like she wasn't telling me the whole truth. She fiddled with a chunky ring on her index finger, twisting it around and around. "I'll count on seeing you tomorrow afternoon so you can meet my friends, 'kay?"

"All right." I turned to leave and soon I was on my way back home. Not as many people were out now as there had been earlier, but I had learned years ago that a city, especially a larger one like this, never truly sleeps. At all hours of the night, people could still be seen out of doors. I was one of those people, but not the only one. I was pretty sure I had violated Mom's rule of returning within an hour. On top of that, she never would have let me leave if she'd known I was making the long trek here.

I eyed the shadows in an alley as I passed it, hastening my pace even though the sidewalk I was on was very brightly lit. Mom didn't like me being in the city alone, especially at night, and ever since I was old enough to be outdoors by myself, she had forbidden it. But for some reason, I simply couldn't keep away from that particular park.

A breath of chilly air drew a sudden violent shiver from me, and now I wished I had thought to bring something warmer than my lightweight denim jacket. Cramming my hands into both coat pockets, I jabbed the knuckles of my left hand against the object inside that pocket.

My fingers brushed against the cool metal of the pen I had found in the park. On a whim, I pulled it from the confines of my pocket, marveling at its sleek exterior. Without realizing it, I had used it when I added to my list of words earlier. As I withdrew my writing journal, I dodged a couple taking a late night stroll and opened the journal to the page I had unsuccessfully tried to fill before. Deep in thought, I let the pen touch the paper as I walked. I often write as I walk, just as some people read books or check messages on their phones. In fact, I had done it so many times before that I quickened my steps, confident in my navigating abilities.

A sentence came to me so suddenly that I came to an abrupt halt, standing motionless in the middle of the sidewalk. Someone bumped into me from behind, then muttered angrily and pushed past me without apologizing. People sidestepped me and a small group momentarily swallowed me as I stood still, letting everyone flow past. Quickly, before I had the chance to forget it, I wrote the line down: *Faith Gray was a dreamer, which was not a desired trait for a Puritan girl in the year 1692.*

Then the words came to me in a flood. My hand flew across the page as I moved the pen as fast as I could, but it wasn't nearly fast enough. As I walked, I held my notebook open with one hand while gripping my pen in the other. Barely noticing the strange looks I was getting, I stopped just long enough to turn the page of my notebook. The story I had been thinking about for months was finally coming out onto the page. It was pouring out of me, and I marveled at it. In all my years of writing, I had never experienced a feeling quite like this.

I let the words fall onto the page, not paying attention to them individually, but rather as a whole. It started to feel as if I wasn't just scratching out lines that turned into letters on the page anymore. It was as if the pen was a vessel for my ideas, setting them forth in black and white.

Somehow, my ideas became more real once they were written on paper. As I wrote, my thoughts were spun into a story, and my characters grew from ink. There was Faith Gray, who was just a bit younger than I was. She wanted to see things beyond her family's house in a village. She longed to see the world, which she knew was so much bigger than the one she and her parents lived in. Her overprotective parents wouldn't let her set foot outside her doorstep alone. Faith was a girl who was expected to be silent and do what she was told, but who, more than anything, yearned to be heard.

My concentration on my writing was so great that I didn't see the metal pole in front of me until I collided with it. A sharp pain struck my forehead and my vision turned blurry as my head began to throb. I stopped writing and reached up to feel a lump the size of a goose egg. Gritting my teeth against the pain, I turned away from the pole.

"Hey! Watch where you're going!"

Stammering a quiet apology, I stumbled away from the annoyed older man I had just bumped into. I was distracted. My writing was messing with my mind, and I couldn't think clearly. I had never felt like this before, and I wasn't sure what it meant.

Scanning the pages of my notebook, I inhaled sharply. My writing was slanted and cramped, nearly running off the page in my haste to get all my thoughts down on paper. It looked nothing like my normally meticulous handwriting. How was this possible? I didn't know how fast I had been writing, but I had been caught in a sort of frenzy, only jarred out of it by a hit to the head.

The words were actually *good*. These were the words I had been striving for months to find. They fit my story perfectly, and every single one seemed to fall into place. I shook my head, too tired to think straight.

Finally, I entered our neighborhood and the sight of my house focused my attention on my approaching predicament: Mom would be furious. The bells of a church a few miles away tolled, and I paused to count them. *One…two…* Before the distant bells ceased, I counted twelve rings. It was midnight. I quickened my pace, clutching my notebook to my chest in an effort not to leave it behind.

Two lights were still on inside our house. One was a single, dim glow near the front of the house on the first floor. I let out an unintentional groan. Mom had stayed up. She would be in the living room with the lamp on, waiting for me to come home.

The other light was no surprise. It came from a window of the upper part of the house. The room was brightly illuminated, and even from several houses away I could see Dad through the glass, staring intently at his canvas, which was mounted on his old wooden easel with the broken foot.

As I climbed the front steps of our house, I stuffed my pen in my pocket and closed my notebook. I wasn't quite sure why, but I didn't want Mom to see what I had written just yet. I pulled my hand out of my warm pocket and exposed it to the bitter night air to grab the door handle, but before I could turn it the door opened on its own, and I came face to face with Mom.

"Where have you been?" Her voice was low and calm, and I was taken aback. I had prepared myself for her irritation and anger, but I wasn't expecting this. The lines on Mom's face were more deeply etched than usual, and my fatigue was reflected in her eyes. A lump formed in my throat. I shouldn't have stayed out so late and made Mom worry. I needed to focus more on the real world instead of getting caught up in my own fantasies.

Mom's eyes flitted first to my hands, which were smeared and stained black with ink. I dropped my arms down, folding my hands together in an attempt to hide the ink. Ridiculous, considering she was already aware of what I had been doing the entire time I was out. She knew my habits too well.

"Oh my goodness, Tess!" Mom's stony gaze melted and she stared at me wide-eyed, her mouth agape. "What on earth happened to your head?"

"Oh." What would be the best way to explain this? That I walked straight into a lamppost in the city, which was exactly where she didn't want me to be, especially at night? "I, uh, I was clumsy."

Maladroit

I half smiled, proud of myself for thinking of that word. Maybe I'd write it down later with the others I collected. "I'm sorry, Mom. I'm okay, really. I promise I won't stay out late at the park anymore."

"The park?" Mom's brow furrowed, and I quickly realized my mistake. "There aren't any parks around here. Where—Tess! You know I don't want you to be in the city at night."

At her withering gaze I drew back from Mom, unable to meet her eyes.

"You're right about one thing, young lady. You won't be going to that park again anytime soon—or anywhere else for that matter. You'll be staying right here for a while."

I looked at her in disbelief. "You mean I'm grounded?" I hadn't been grounded since I was seven, when I punched a girl in my class for calling me vile. I doubted she knew what the word really meant at the time, but to me that was a horrific thing to call somebody.

I wasn't seven years old anymore, but Mom knew how much I preferred to be outside while I wrote about my surroundings. It was the worst kind of punishment for someone like me.

"That's right," Mom said in response to my question.

I stared at her, not missing the completely serious expression on her face. She didn't think I could take care of myself, because I didn't interact with other people as much as I should. But she was wrong. I'd read many, many books, which prepared me for life almost as well as living it did.

Once I realized she was not going to give in, I nodded in resignation. "Fine." I trudged up the stairs to my room, where I would try my best to get some rest.

Tucked beneath the covers, I stared at the darkness surrounding me. I tried reciting the entries in my dictionary alphabetically, but it was no use — no matter how drowsy I was, I could not fall asleep. Wriggling out of the sheets tangled around my legs, I put on my slippers and padded over to my desk in the darkness. I switched on an overhead lamp and took a seat.

My notebook sat where I had left it on the smooth surface of my desk, the golden pen wedged between two pages to mark my spot. I let my fingers graze the cover of the notebook, feeling each ridge in the shiny blue leather. After several moments' hesitation, I opened the book to the place where I had left off.

An inexplicable sensation arose in my chest. I knew this feeling — the feeling of needing to write. But would the words still flow the way they had somehow done earlier? What if they no longer came so effortlessly?

I put my pen to the page, trying to hold it steady in my quivering hand. As soon as I formed the first word, all my doubts were erased.

The words were as fluent as before, but this time my writing wasn't as frantic. It was a steady flow of thoughts translated onto paper, and although my hand was constantly moving, I no longer wrote at breakneck speed. The words weren't going anywhere.

They were in my head — they had been all along — and now they were pouring out.

Success

I couldn't contain the smile that spread across my face. I had grown so used to failure that I had forgotten what it felt like to succeed.

I wrote late into the night, with words on my mind and at my fingertips. And when I rested my head on my arms as the night waned and faint light began to creep across the floor, words filled my dreams too.

Chapter Three

It was baffling how the words surged through my pen and didn't let up until I was too exhausted to write them anymore.

Enigma

Turning to the back of my notebook, I added the word to the bottom of the short list. I ran my hands over the letters, as if I could actually feel a raised impression of each line and curve. The list included four words that I had chosen years ago.

Glitter

Skip

Grotesque

Pink

I had chosen *grotesque* because I liked how it sounded on my tongue and looked on the page. *Pink* made the list when I saw a particularly beautiful sunset when I was nine and couldn't think of a better way to describe it than pink, which, at that time, seemed to say it all.

So far I had collected a dozen words that all had their own special meanings for me, even though some were simple, everyday words that meant nothing to most people. For all I knew, I would keep on collecting words for the rest of my life. There were only a few words I deemed good enough to keep when I was younger, but recently my list had been growing faster than ever before.

While other kids had imaginary friends that they talked to when they were little, I had my words, which were more real to me anyway. Now, I simply whispered the words to myself, if only to see whether they still held the same power over me that they had when I'd first chosen them. They always did.

Lexicon

Words soothed me when there was no one else around to do so. With an endless supply of words, I knew I would never run out. Though I did worry that eventually my words would lose their individual significance. I was a collector of words, but what would I do with them once there were too many to count and remember? There was no way to know.

Conundrum

I spent all of Saturday morning working on the story I had started the night before, researching the time period so everything would be just right. I knew I wanted my main character, Faith, to live in colonial America in the year 1692, a time in history marked by the Salem Witch Trials that devastated a town in Massachusetts.

I was fascinated by the little I had learned of this event in history class the year before, so I was eager to find out more about that period. I would have preferred doing my research using the library's books, newspaper articles, and sketches, but the Internet would have to suffice, as Mom had not agreed to lift my grounding.

As I pored over pages and pages of online articles and websites, my eyes flitted from one side of the computer screen to the other. So much information, so many possibilities. I took a deep breath, pulling my shoulder-length blond hair out of my face and securing it in a loose knot at the back of my head, and tried to focus on the basics first.

It began in 1692 in Salem, in what was then the Massachusetts Bay Colony. Dozens of young Puritan girls who lived there suddenly succumbed to a mysterious disease, their bodies convulsing as they fell to the floor in terrible fits. Desperate to assuage their pain, the town officials begged the girls to tell them what was causing their suffering. The girls cried out that it was witches — their own neighbors — that pinched them and slashed at their skin. The townspeople believed them. They had to, after witnessing the terrible afflictions that only the Devil could have caused. More and more witches were discovered, tried, and ultimately hanged — neighbors and friends who swore that they were innocent. The hangings continued, but still the girls' conditions grew worse as the Witch Trials frenzy spread.

It's an intriguing, horrible story. But what is most baffling is that even now, centuries later, no one knows for sure why the girls suddenly began seeing witches. Some people think the girls were simply pretending to be tormented because they were bored with their everyday lives. Others believe the girls really did fall ill. The controversy was the reason I wanted to use that setting in my story. My curiosity about this period in history grew into a need to understand how it could have happened.

The smell of bacon wafted up from the kitchen. Because there would have to be a big event for Mom to cook two consecutive meals, she must have been heating a microwaveable brunch for herself, which she often did because it took less effort. Although she wasn't teaching today, I knew she would look through the projects the kids had done during the week and organize materials for the following week, as she always did. Mom and I didn't have the greatest relationship with each other, but I still felt a twinge of pain when I saw her spend so much time with the kids she taught. When was the last time she had really spent time with me? Sometimes it felt like her students were closer to Mom than I was.

Exhaling heavily, I closed my laptop and pushed it aside. Words, words, *words*. As usual, I couldn't stop thinking about them. I turned to the back of my notebook and absentmindedly scrawled *words* at the bottom of my list. If any single word had an effect on my life, that one was it.

Words

I spent the rest of the morning and part of the afternoon writing continuously, only stopping for a few bites to eat when Mom began yelling for Dad and me to come down for lunch so loudly that I could no longer ignore her. If my parents noticed my blank, faraway expression, they didn't mention it. I was certain that Dad didn't notice. He was staring out the window with a contemplative look on his face, and he appeared much the same as I imagined I probably did.

Back in my room a few minutes later, I resumed writing. By now, the ink that I inevitably got on my hands each time I wrote was encrusted and dried around my fingernails, and there was a thin, hardened layer all along the side of my right hand. The ink was a permanent part of me, as it had been for quite some time, and though at one time I might have been able to scrub it off, I doubted I could now, even if I tried.

As the story grew, my handwriting became smaller and overflowed into the margins of the paper in an effort to fit more words on each page. My blue leather notebook which I'd had for years was filling up quickly, and I feared that it would be filled completely before I was finished. I suppose I could have written the story on my computer, but I took some satisfaction in seeing the words written in my own handwriting.

Ink

It was more real to me than any illuminated electronic device that could erase the whole story unintentionally with one click of the mouse.

I was finished writing, for the time being. The story wasn't complete yet, and I wasn't sure exactly how it would end, but I hoped I would discover that later on. I had used both historical figures and fictional characters in my story, and they had all become real to me: Reverend Samuel Parris, Ann Putnam Jr., Bridget Sutton, and of course, my main character, Faith.

I could picture Faith in my mind—I always had been able to—and now my mental image of her was even clearer than it had been before. Unlike me, she didn't know what she wanted from life, except that she wanted to *live*. Faith wanted to see the world, not just the little corner of it that she had been kept in her entire life.

Wanderlust

Something flashed and filled my vision, momentarily blinding me. "Mom? Hazel?" I looked around my room. Everything was how it was supposed to be, from the blue rug that covered the ugly brown carpet at the foot of my bed to the bookshelves mounted on the wall that held my encyclopedias, dictionaries, and other reference books. Nothing was out of place. *I could have sworn…*

My desk became blurry around the edges, and I blinked several times successively, trying to regain the clarity of my normal vision. It didn't help — everything seemed hazy. Maybe I had something stuck in my eyes.

I started to rise from my chair, but when I stood, a bout of lightheadedness overtook me and I stumbled, grasping the back of my chair for balance. The blurriness had grown, and now all I could see was indistinct light and color. I closed my eyes, desperately willing it all to stop, but letters began to fly across the backs of my eyelids. They formed words, words I couldn't quite comprehend. Jumbled and strange, I couldn't quite make out what they said.

Another wave of dizziness shook me, and then I was on my knees, squeezing my eyes tightly shut.

What was going on? Pain erupted throughout my body and a strangled cry came from my throat. There was a sound like a terrible ripping — of paper, cloth, skin, I didn't know.

Then without warning, the pain eased, leaving only a tingling sensation running up and down my arms. Cautiously I opened my eyes, ready to survey any damage to my room, but something was terribly wrong. I wasn't where I had been just a few moments ago.

The carpet I had been kneeling on mere seconds — or had it been hours? — ago was replaced by slightly muddy ground. What was going on here? When I clenched my hands, dragging my fingers through the mud and collecting much of it beneath my fingernails, I realized I was sprawled on the ground. It must have been a dirt road, because the dirt was packed and trodden on, and it seemed to follow a generally straight line.

I had just registered the many intermingled voices around me when a loud rattling rose above the other sounds. Glancing up, I recoiled in alarm and struggled to get into a sitting position. A horse pulling a wooden wagon came hurtling down the road straight toward me, much too fast.

The breath caught in my throat and my body froze as the horse thundered closer. My alarm turned to panic. I tried to fling myself to the side, but my legs would not cooperate with me. Dirt and mud flew everywhere as the wagon rapidly gained on me, its driver trying unsuccessfully to slow it down. I was going to be trampled. The large beast's hooves were inches away from me.

In the split second before the rearing legs of the horse struck me, I felt a hand on my arm, and I was yanked sharply to the side. I tumbled and careened into a brick wall, where I finally came to a stop. Each breath I took tore at my throat as I gasped for air.

"Are you well, Miss?" A voice broke through the jumble of thoughts in my mind. I looked up, rapidly blinking to get the sting of dirt out of my eyes. Standing over me was a girl only a few years younger than I. Her brow creased with worry as she spoke. "Mayhap I ought to fetch the physician?"

Her words confused me. "What?" I let my head fall back against the sturdy wall of the building behind me. Was I delirious? Why else would she be speaking so strangely?

The girl wore a dark dress with a large white collar. The dress had a full skirt that nearly reached her ankles, leaving her brown, buckled shoes exposed. Her head was covered by a white cap that hid most of her hair, although a dark brown wisp hung down from her forehead. She must have been dressed up for a costume party. Her costume was so authentic, I couldn't help but admire it. Or maybe she was part of a reenactment our town was organizing. That would explain the old-fashioned way she spoke. I decided that idea was better than accepting the possibility that I had gone crazy.

I looked up at the girl and realized she was still waiting for me to respond. "No, I'm okay." She just looked back at me in bewilderment. Her eyes were a very clear blue, and there was something about her face that reminded me of someone I knew. Cocking my head, I examined her face even closer. "Do I know you?"

The girl shook her head, eyes narrowed in confusion. "Are you a newcomer to this town? I am afraid I do not recognize you." She held out a hand, and I placed mine in hers. It took me a moment to realize she meant to pull me up to a standing position, not shake hands like I had awkwardly tried to do.

Choking back a laugh, I answered her. "I've lived here my whole life." How could she expect to know everyone in a town of tens of thousands of people? I got to my feet too quickly, and a spasm of dizziness made me sway.

The girl reached out to steady me, grasping my arm. When I regained my balance she let me go, leaving half-moon shaped fingernail marks on my skin.

I gazed at her, taking in her rumpled dress and the smudge of dirt smeared across one cheek. Surely I looked worse. My thoughts were sluggish and I hoped I didn't have a concussion.

Muddled

"Oh!" I realized suddenly. "You're the one that saved me. You pulled me away from that horse, didn't you? Thank you."

The girl frowned. "Think nothing of it. Anyone would have done the same." She blinked, regarding me with a bewildered expression. "What strange attire," she murmured under her breath, her words barely audible.

"Ann! Come over here!" A group of girls, all dressed similarly, beckoned to her from across the street, standing next to a long, white, wooden building. Ann waved to them, then turned to me.

"I must go now. Are you quite sure you are all right?"

"Uh, y-yes. Thank you again," I stumbled over my words.

"Very well." Ann brushed the stray wisp of hair from her forehead and hurried over to her friends, who laughed and entered the building together, leaving me completely alone outside.

That was when I allowed my panic to set in. This was *not* my town. Streets that should have been paved were made of dirt. Instead of cars and trucks, wagons seemed to be the only wheeled mode of transportation. Nothing was how it was supposed to be. I didn't know how I had ended up in this place and, right now, I wanted more than anything to be back in my room.

But what if I *hadn't* left my room? This could all be a dream. Any time now I could wake up, feeling silly for thinking that something as irrational as this could be real. I'd have a good laugh with Hazel about my hyperactive imagination.

It was easier to believe that I was dreaming than to accept the fact that all of this was real.

I began to walk, if only to gain composure and give myself something to do. As I passed the building I had bumped into, I turned to get a better look. It was a prominent, stately structure with steps up to the highly adorned entrance. A metal plaque fixed to one wall was partially covered by a patch of ivy. From this angle, the only visible word on the sign was "Courthouse."

I started toward the building, intending to see what the rest of the sign said, but a sudden eerie silence came over the place. Surveying the area around me, I looked up and down the street, finding that the inhabitants who had been here only a few moments ago were now gone. The sounds of clattering wagon wheels and quiet voices no longer drifted over to me. Only the howling of the wind remained.

Unsettled, I quickened my pace, passing many buildings but not seeing another soul. A frigid wind arose, making me shiver and hunch over to keep warm. I couldn't remember the last time it had been so cold in September. Why couldn't I have at least been wearing something heavier than my threadbare denim jacket when I appeared here?

My limbs ached, and I knew without looking that I was covered with bruises from my tumble. I felt as if my body had been drained of energy, yet I kept moving.

The buildings became more scattered and less frequent as I stumbled on. Battered boards creaked beneath my feet as I crossed a bridge that stretched across a narrow river. The water was frozen over, a sheet of ice stretching in both directions as far as I could see.

It was only September. Something wasn't right.

The wind blew strands of hair in my face, and I brushed them away. My fingers were numb with cold, and I flexed them to make the uncontrollable tingling stop.

Stiffening, I came to a standstill. I was wandering. I knew it, but I couldn't make myself stop.

Adrift

The sky overhead was darkening, and sporadic eruptions of clouds marred the otherwise clear expanse, making the sky seem almost angry. It hadn't been like this before, I was certain. Just how much time had passed?

In the back of my mind something nagged at me. I was forgetting something important. What was it that I needed to remember?

I recognized none of my surroundings. This wasn't my town—I knew that now without a doubt. My heartbeat quickened, and I struggled to move faster. I was disoriented and confused, but this didn't feel like a dream. Whatever had happened, I needed to find help—and shelter. The bitter cold air pierced my skin like thousands of needles, and my toes had gone numb. Every second I lingered meant an increasing risk of frostbite or hypothermia.

Just then I reached the top of a grassy mound.

Zenith

The hill was large enough to have an impact on the surrounding terrain, but it wasn't difficult to climb.

A tiny wooden house sat just beneath the hill. A central chimney protruded from a roof covered in what appeared to be wooden shingles. The house was only one story tall, and it couldn't have had more than a few rooms. It was one of the smallest houses I had ever seen—it reminded me a little bit of our neighbor's shed that he kept in his backyard.

Other buildings were scattered beyond. This must be another town, although it looked more like a small village. Unlike the first town with the courthouse and adorned buildings, this village was rustic. Most of the houses were small and sported shabby wooden shingles, and the more dilapidated structures had thatched roofs. The dirt roads that threaded through this community were less defined and hardly wide enough to fit two wagons side by side. Yells resounded in the area as a group of children darted around a house and across the road. One of them stopped suddenly and looked over his shoulder at where I stood on the hill. His eyes grew round and he turned on his heel and raced into a house, disappearing inside.

Shaking my head, I started to move when a few white flakes drifted down and landed on my skin, melting instantly. Within moments the snow picked up, creating a web of snowflakes in my hair. The bitter cold air felt good against my face now, and the flakes swirled around me. Watching them made me dizzy.

Then without warning the snow fell harder and faster, until the flurries became a blizzard. Head down, I fought my way through the storm, running blindly. The earth beneath me had become slick and I stumbled, catching myself. I was cold to the core. My sneakers were soaked and soggy. Oh, what I wouldn't give right now for clothing that was a bit more waterproof.

It was difficult to see where I was going. The sky had turned dark with the arrival of the storm clouds, but I managed to reach the little house at the base of the hill. My breath came in ragged gasps. Exhausted, I put my fist to the door and rapped on the wood, praying whoever was inside would take pity on me and let me in to dry off, if only for a few minutes.

The door opened to reveal a little boy peeking out at me with bright eyes. Although he looked very young, he was dressed like a man, with the same strange attire as everyone else I had seen so far. The tall stovepipe hat perched on his head looked comical on someone as small and young as he was. He smiled at me shyly, though his eyes probed my soaked hair and clothes with curiosity and interest. I opened my mouth to speak, but the boy turned away from me. "Mother, it is a girl at our doorstep! She is all wet!"

A thin, middle-aged woman came to the door and peered out at me quizzically. Only her eyes registered her surprise at my appearance. "Come, come inside, child, and hurry now!" She ushered me into the house and I followed in relief, eager to get out of the blizzard.

As I entered, my sneakers made squelching

noises with each step. Melting snow dripped in a trail behind me, and small puddles began to accumulate on the uneven wooden floor.

I could feel the intensity of several pairs of eyes fixed upon me. The mother was still standing at my side anxiously, twisting a bit of her dress around her finger over and over again. The little boy who had opened the door was running around the room, flailing his arms about in excitement until his mother shushed him.

The two other people in the room appraised me as well. A man with scruffy red hair, who must have been the father, regarded me solemnly from his position at a table in the center of the room. I tried to give him a friendly smile, but, if anything, his grim expression just intensified. Beside him stood a girl around my age. Her face was scrubbed clean and her dark brown hair was pulled back into a tight bun at the nape of her neck. A starched, stiff cap covered the rest of her hair. She offered me a small but warm smile, which, after a moment, I returned.

With everyone's eyes on me, I couldn't think straight. The room had fallen silent, but before long the woman broke the silence, visibly relieving the tension in the room. "Do have supper with us, child. We were nearly ready when you arrived." She gestured at the small square table in the middle of the room, where the girl and father were positioned. Only now did I notice the bowls of food and plates set out. The room we all stood in must have been the main room, serving as both the living room and kitchen. Against one wall stood a fireplace with a large hearth, where a bulky black pot hung over a crackling fire—no doubt where they cooked their food. If this was some kind of reenactment, it was going too far.

The woman misinterpreted my silence as indecision. "I would offer you a dry dress to don to get you out of your wet clothes, but I am afraid we have no spare clothing. What a shame, for you are the same size as my daughter."

"Oh!" I glanced down at my jeans and denim jacket that were weighed down with water. "No, that's all right, I completely understand. I would…love to eat with you, but I don't want to, um, intrude."

The man with the red hair rose, his chair scraping violently against the floor, and spoke for the first time since I had arrived. "We are a God-fearing family," he said in a booming voice, as if that were explanation enough. "We help those around us, and none shall remain hungry in our midst. We do not turn anyone away." His seriousness never wavered, and his words were completely sincere.

"Thank you." The family gathered around the table in the center of the room, and I waited until the woman looked over her shoulder and motioned for me to do so as well.

As I followed them to the table, I scuffed my shoes on the floor. The planks of wood had been sanded and fit closely together, but the wood was unpainted and the cracks between the floorboards were conspicuous. The room was sparsely furnished. Besides the fireplace and table, the room contained only a cupboard, several chairs, a stool, and pegs on the walls where hats and coats hung. There was a single window by the door I had come in, but I couldn't see out of it. Upon closer inspection, I realized it had no glass. Instead, it was covered with oiled paper.

A persistent dripping had begun, causing me to look away from the window. Water was seeping from a crack that cut across the ceiling. "Oh, it is such a bother!" the woman exclaimed in frustration. "William, pray, fetch the bucket by the hearth and place it beneath the leak." When the boy didn't look up from the string he was knotting over and over again, his mother grew frustrated. "Will!"

At the sound of his mother calling his nickname, the little boy scurried over and slid an empty bucket over several feet, where it caught the melting snow that seeped through the hole in the roof. William returned to the table, where he stood next to his sister, who was watching me with unconcealed interest.

"Here." The mother showed me to the spot at the table that was closest to the fireplace. When I dragged a vacant chair over and sat down, the woman let out an audible gasp and I looked up, startled. The red-haired man across from me eyed me sternly, but the girl hid a smile. When she saw I was watching, she gave me a grin, as if we shared a secret. I grimaced. Had I done something wrong? For some reason, William and his sister were both still standing, but their parents were both seated. Maybe I had grabbed the wrong chair.

Finally William piped up. "Children must not sit at the table unless asked, and not until after the blessing!" he informed me, giggling. "That is what Mother always says."

Oh. My cheeks flushed and I rocketed up from the chair, nearly tipping it over, but the mother shook her head. "No, no. You are our guest, and you are weary. Pray, do sit." With hesitation, I did as she bid me. The heat from the fireplace warmed my back, and I let out a long breath. It felt good to be out of the storm. I still didn't understand what was going on, but at least I was no longer shivering.

"Daughter, do say grace for us." The red-haired man's low voice startled me. The girl looked taken aback. She fidgeted under her father's gaze but after a moment nodded.

Everyone bowed their heads, and I did the same, though I watched the girl from the corner of my eye.

"Dear Lord," the girl began, her voice quavering ever so slightly, "We thank thee for thy food thou hast given us and pray that thou bless our family and neighbors in this time of misfortune." She spoke quietly, but her voice startled me. Hadn't I heard that voice somewhere before? The familiarity of it was uncanny.

Oblivious that I was hardly listening, the girl continued on. "Deliver us from the evil that has befallen this town, and—" Here she stopped for a moment, looking up at her mother, who gave her a stern look and tilted her head in my direction.

"And we thank thee for the company of this girl who thou hast led to our doorstep. Amen," she finished abruptly, and we all echoed, "Amen."

Her mother didn't look pleased at the brevity of the prayer. Her eyes were narrowed, and I had no doubt that she would reprimand her daughter when I was not within hearing distance.

The girl passed me a plate that her mother had already filled. All it held was a biscuit, a dollop of something resembling pudding, and a chunk of meat. I dove right into my biscuit, devouring it as quickly as I could without seeming rude. How long had it been since I had eaten? I'd lost all sense of time, and with the storm still raging outside I couldn't tell how late it was.

The biscuit was hard and golden on the outside, but the inside was flaky and fresh. Somehow it almost melted in my mouth. I had never eaten anything that tasted so good.

Ethereal

The meat, though, was trickier. I had been given a spoon for the pudding, but no other utensils. To my right, William and his sister still stood, sharing the food on a single plate. William stuffed the meat into his mouth with his bare hands, and I waited to see if this would anger his mother, but no admonishment came. She, too, was eating the meat with her bare hands, albeit in a more refined manner. As I looked around the table discreetly, I realized everyone did the same. Imitating the mother, I took the whole chunk of meat in my hands and tried to bite off a dainty piece. The meat was greasy and tough, and it was covered in fat. The taste wasn't bad, but it wasn't like the meat I was used to eating.

"Does the duck meat please you?" the red-haired man asked me, and I nearly choked on the morsel in my mouth. "We had some extra from our midday meal."

We were eating duck? It took an enormous effort to swallow what was in my mouth. "Um, it's very delicious." I didn't want to offend anybody.

"Dear me, we have neglected to introduce

ourselves," the mother said suddenly. "We are the Gray family. Where have you come from...?" Mrs. Gray trailed off, looking at me questioningly. She was waiting for my name.

"Tess," I filled in. Everyone looked up from their food except for William, who was busy shredding his meat into tiny pieces with his fingers. "I, uh, just passed through a town not far from here. Maybe you know what it is?"

The red-haired man, Mr. Gray, spoke up. "Ah, yes, we know the town you speak of. It is Salem Town."

"Salem Town?" There weren't any towns by that name where I lived. Dread filled the pit of my stomach.

"Yes. And we are in Salem Village. Did you not know that?"

I shook my head, trying to make sense of it all. At my silence, Mr. Gray continued. "Yes, Salem Village of Massachusetts Bay Colony."

Massachusetts Bay Colony. Suddenly, a sour taste filled my mouth, and it felt as though there was something stuck in my throat. "What is today's date?"

Mrs. Gray answered this time. "Why, it is the twenty-eighth of January, of course."

No, it wasn't. It was September thirtieth. Panic began to fill me, and my breath came faster. "What year?" My voice came out as a low whisper.

Mrs. Gray gave me a funny look. "Are you quite

all right, child? Today is January twenty-eighth, in the year of our Lord, 1692."

Chapter Four

I was in shock. It was 1692. I could tell by the look on Mrs. Gray's face that she was not kidding. I wasn't in the middle of a historical reenactment—this was real.

How had this happened? Was it possible that I had traveled through time unknowingly? Wouldn't I have needed a time machine? Was there something else going on here? I groaned to myself. I was in way over my head.

Inundated

Most of the remaining part of the meal was spent in silence, except for one point when Mrs. Gray commented that Tess was such an unusual name. I didn't think it was, really, but when I explained it stood for Therese she seemed pleased, saying that it was a good Christian name, and she seemed to forget my strange behavior.

After the meal, Mrs. Gray scrubbed the dishes while her husband sat by the fireplace reading a thick, black book that was surely the Bible. The girl, who had hardly spoken a word to me before, pulled me outside, closing the door firmly behind her. "You spoke earlier that you passed through Salem Town. Are you traveling a great distance? Do you travel alone?" Her tone was respectful, but her sparkling eyes gave away her interest.

"Uh…yes, I am," I answered. If I really had traveled back in time, it would be better to keep my answers vague. Besides, technically I was telling the truth. I had been alone, and it seemed like I had traveled across the country, back three centuries — all in the blink of an eye.

"Mercy, what an adventure it must be! How do you do it? What is it like? Where have you been? Oh, I have so many questions!" As the girl spoke, her reserved expression became enraptured, and she gestured excitedly with her hands. Her cap came loose and hung askew, revealing her shiny dark hair, but she hardly seemed to notice.

I gaped at her, but I couldn't seem to make myself look away. Where had I seen her before? She seemed so familiar to me, like she was a neighbor or someone

I had seen in the city. But that was impossible. Then again, being here in the year 1692 should also be impossible. So, why did I recognize her face?

I started to open my mouth to ask her name, but sudden nausea swept through my body, forcing me to ease myself onto the ground before I collapsed.

Vertigo

The girl bent down over me, a concerned expression on her face. She was saying something to me, but I could no longer hear her voice. *Oh no*, I thought, *please, no. Not again.*

My surroundings split into different colors and blurred, and I was suddenly glad I was sitting down, because I no longer knew which way was up. Spots filled my vision and another wave of nausea hit me. The girl was still in front of me, but she turned toward the house and yanked open the door, calling out for her mother. Dizziness overtook me, and the last thing I saw before I lost my sight was the girl staring at me, a horrified expression on her face.

This time, I hadn't closed my eyes, I was sure of it. When the dizziness had almost become too much, I saw nothing, not even darkness, yet I knew my eyes were open when I blinked. Then my vision returned, and colors and light flooded into my eyes. I was kneeling on familiar, ugly brown carpet, next to a desk and chair.

I stood slowly, my knees wobbling a bit from the effort to hold myself up, and as I turned in a circle to survey the room, my eyes widened in disbelief. There was my bed, with my old ratty blanket spread over it and the many pillows that nearly covered the upper half, my blue and green rag rug, my dresser, and my shelf of encyclopedias. I was back in my room.

But maybe I had never left it.

That one thought tugged at my mind, not letting me think of anything else. It was easy to dismiss the events of the day as nothing more than a crazy dream. I was relieved, but also a little disappointed. Most of all though, I was just confused. Everything had seemed so real.

Illusions

Moving toward my window, I tried to look out but couldn't see anything. Night had fallen. I checked the wall clock that hung above my door — 9:15. I must have been asleep for hours, missing most of the afternoon and evening.

I slipped out of my room and into a quiet hallway, anxious to see what I had missed. Mom was probably very annoyed that I had failed to attend dinner again, but she had evidently decided to let me be.

Instead of heading downstairs to the kitchen, I turned in the opposite direction and found myself in front of the door to Dad's studio. Not surprisingly, a light shone from the crack beneath the door. He was working late again.

I knocked on the door, half-expecting Dad to be so caught up in his work that he wouldn't answer, which happened sometimes, but after a moment the door swung open and Dad grinned at me from inside. "Hey there, Tess! Come on in." He disappeared inside the room again, and I followed. I hadn't been sure he would let me inside anymore. I wondered when the last time was that Mom had been in the room either.

Art supplies littered the floor, and most of the furniture was covered with discarded canvases and papers, which I knew were past artistic endeavors. The surface of every piece of furniture that was not covered sported a thick layer of dust. In addition, paint splotches dotted the floor. It was a good thing that the room was tiled rather than carpeted. I stepped around a particularly large spill of red acrylic paint.

Disarray

Dodging several stacks of boxes, I made my way over to the far corner and perched myself on the edge of a stool by a table and an easel that was smaller than the others that were always set up. I couldn't believe they were still here.

When I was younger, I used to come in here and paint with Dad. At first I used finger paint, and then I graduated to crayons and colored pencils. When I got a bit older, Dad let me try out his watercolors. Since then, he had kept out the little easel and drawing supplies in one corner for me.

Reminisce

The mediocre paintings I had created were hanging on the walls around the room—not just above my easel, but all over—whereas everything Dad created himself was rejected and thrown into a pile on the ground.

"What are you making today, Dad?"

He had seated himself on the other side of the room at his favorite easel, where the light from the moon found its way in from the window. He didn't answer for a moment, but then he turned from his easel to face me. "I'll show you if you promise not to tell your mother."

He hadn't let me see any of his paintings in a long time. I nodded quickly and came to his side when he beckoned me closer. A half-finished watercolor was clipped to the easel. It was a partially formed portrait of a dark-haired woman from the neck up. Her hair was loose, and the face was mostly formed, but the bottom half of the painting hadn't been completed yet. "It's Mom," I said at once, and Dad laughed.

"Glad she's recognizable at least," he joked, then grew serious. "I can't seem to get the nose right, though…"

I looked closer. The nose was a little wide and wasn't exactly like Mom's. "The painting looks beautiful so far, though." Dad only stared at the easel impassively. "I don't think you should throw it away this time."

"I never throw any of my paintings away." Dad gestured to a pile of thick papers and canvases in the middle of the room. They were all face-down, and the papers were crumpled into tiny balls. One of the canvases had a gaping hole through the middle.

Forlorn

I turned away from the disturbing image. "What were those paintings of? The ones you discarded?"

"Maybe I'll tell you sometime." Dad gazed at the semi-formed face of Mom without really seeing it, obviously distracted. Then he straightened. "Let's get to work."

I wandered over to my corner and sat down again, absentmindedly scratching the birthmark on my arm. Trying not to think about what had happened today, I picked up a pencil and began to draw quick, sharp lines on a piece of paper from a stack on the table. It wasn't working. I had told myself repeatedly that the events of today were nothing more than a dream, but I wasn't so sure I could really believe that. It was all so confusing. I couldn't get the images of Salem Town, the Gray family, and especially that girl out of my head. I kept feeling that strange sense that I had been there before, and I couldn't seem to shake it away.

Déjà vu

The phrase was French, but the words flowed so nicely together and had earned their meaning in the English language. I'd add them to my list later.

Returning my attention to my sketch, I added a few lines here and there and shaded in one side with the edge of the pencil. Drawing didn't affect me the way writing did. I could lose myself in the power of words in a way that I couldn't with any other activity.

They say a picture is worth a thousand words, and while that's probably true, I felt that there was more to it than that. I believed that a single word could evoke thousands of pictures. Words meant more to me than anything, and I could pluck them out and find them in the places around me. But I couldn't put words into a drawing or a painting. There was only one way I knew to express myself, and that was by writing.

I stood up abruptly, startling Dad. "Can I see?" He held out a hand for the drawing I was clutching. I supposed it was only fair, since he had shown me his artwork. I offered him the paper and he took it, staring at it for several long moments while I shifted from one foot to the other.

"Very good," he told me finally. "The shading looks accurate, but the eyes seem a little too big in proportion to the rest of the face."

I only nodded, quite used to his advice. I would have minded more if he was critiquing my writing. My words were so personal to me. They were my creations and I couldn't bear the thought of them being examined by those I was close to—at least not yet.

"Is this someone you know?"

"Yes." And it was, sort of. I had drawn the girl from Salem as I remembered her, whether she was real or merely a figment of my overactive imagination. "I think I'll hold on to this for a while." Dad looked a little disappointed that I wasn't going to leave it here, with my other drawings and paintings.

I lingered near the doorway, and before I left Dad called out to me, "Hey, wait a minute. Why are your clothes so wet, honey?" I just looked at him as he continued, "When you first came in I was too preoccupied with my painting to notice, but now I can see you're damp all over."

I looked down at my clothes in astonishment. He was right. My jeans stuck to my skin and the tips of my hair still held a few drops of water. But that couldn't be. A storm in my dreams couldn't soak me. So that could only mean…

Realization

I gasped and dashed from the room, leaving the door to Dad's studio ajar in my hurry. "Don't forget to go downstairs and find your mother!" Dad called after me. "I think we both missed dinner tonight. She got home late from her meeting with the other teacher, but I still don't think she's very happy we've missed another meal."

I yelled back over my shoulder that I would, but I had different intentions. Rounding the corner and reentering my room, I slid into my chair and switched on the overhead light once again. My notebook was lying open on the desktop. Strange. I didn't remember leaving it open. I was always very careful to close it in case Mom got curious during one of her cleaning frenzies.

I immediately turned to the back of the book where I kept my list of words. First, I hurriedly scrawled the words that I had thought of earlier but hadn't had time to write down. Once I wrote the new ones down, I kept going. I had to release the words onto the paper, letting my overwhelming feelings pour out with them. They streamed out onto the page, disjointed and illogical, one after another, each one telling a part of the story of my life.

Believe

Creations

Downpour

Questions

Bright

Insufficient

Wonder

Truth

After I finished lengthening my list, I turned to the page of my story that I was still working on. I hoped that if I continued writing, it would help calm my racing thoughts—let me see more clearly what was real and what was not.

I eased into a steady rhythm as I moved my new pen back and forth across the page. It was almost as if I was writing to music, an unheard beat, but my room was quiet except for the movement of my pen and my hand brushing against the page.

I didn't know how long I had been writing, as time always seemed to get away from me when I wasn't keeping a close eye on it. I had been writing a great deal in the past few days, and my notebook was filling quickly with hastily written pages of the story. My story was growing rapidly too, and I knew the feeling would be bittersweet for me when it came time to part with my characters. It was like that when I read good books, too. I never wanted the stories to end. And Faith Gray was such a likable character.

I froze in my seat, the sudden realization making my muscles go rigid. I couldn't believe it. How had I not understood before? I slammed my clenched fist down on the surface of my desk as hard as I could, barely giving thought to my stinging knuckles. How could I be so stupid?

I turned the pages back in my notebook so quickly that some of them folded and wrinkled under my palm in my haste to reach the beginning of the story.

There it was, staring at me, stark against the page. I had filled the space with descriptions and information about my character, Faith Gray. Who had the same last name as the girl I had met only hours ago. Could that possibly be a coincidence? I didn't think so. There had been too many of them lately for me to believe they weren't all connected to each other.

In my story, there were four members of the Gray family. Just like the family I had met today.

Coincidence

I allowed myself to think for a moment as I absentmindedly formed *coincidence* on a line on the final page of my notebook. The girl had seemed so familiar when I looked at her earlier today. In fact, much of my surroundings had seemed familiar. The girl had never told me her name, but could it be Faith Gray? My story was set in a community called Salem Village. Was it possible that it was the same Salem Village where I had been today?

There was no reason for the girl or anything I had seen today to look familiar. I had never met them before today. And it was not a dream. My damp clothes were proof enough. The conclusion I came to was mind-blowing. What if the place I had been was the setting of my story, and the people that lived there were characters of my own creation? "I made them," I whispered.

No. That thought sounded so ridiculous spoken aloud. I threw my hands into the air in frustration, and then buried my face in them. I could no longer tell reality from fiction.

But I had to check—I had to find out for certain. I flipped a page and read a portion of the detailed character description of my main character, Faith Gray: *follows her parents' wishes, but wants to travel the world.* My breath hitched. That seemed spot on, as far as I could tell. I read on.

Medium height. Straight dk. brown hair always tucked beneath cap. Pale complexion, heart-shaped face, large gray eyes, high forehead.

Slowly, I reached for the sketch I had made of the

girl I had met today, which lay face down on the desk beside me. Almost too afraid to look, I turned it over hesitantly and studied the roughly drawn face that looked back at me steadily.

There was no doubt about it—it was her. I had come face to face with my own character mere hours ago, and she was exactly how I expected her to be.

Chapter Five

I spent the next hour going through my notebook, trying to find more connections between my story and what I had seen today. Yes, there was the courthouse in Salem Town, and the Grays' house followed its description in my story perfectly.

But the people I had seen were harder to identify and match. Faith Gray, of course, was the most notable match and most important to my story, and her family members were recognizable. Not everyone I had seen matched my story, though. The only people I recognized were the Grays, although I had seen crowds of other people in Salem Town. Was it possible that I had brought to life those people too, ones that I hadn't written into the story?

I began to leaf through the pages of notes from

the research I had done to write my story. There were several large blizzards in 1692, but I had not written about a blizzard in my story. Yet I had experienced one today. Also, I had crossed a bridge on my way to Salem Village. I searched a map that had been drawn of historical Salem Village and Salem Town. There were many bridges, and one that looked like it could be the bridge I had crossed, but I had never mentioned a bridge in my writing.

Almost everything I had seen today closely followed what I had learned about history. Maybe I actually had traveled through time. But that didn't explain why Faith Gray and her family looked so familiar. They couldn't be real people from history. Faith and her family were characters of my own invention, rather than ones based on historical figures I had come across in my research. I knew deep down inside that Faith was my own character, and it couldn't be a coincidence that the girl I had met looked like her.

The only explanation I could come to was that something happened when I began writing that story. *Somehow, my story and the past had become connected!*

I couldn't help but wonder at what point in time I had been in Salem. I knew it was during 1692, but so much had happened that year—the date was important. Then I slapped my forehead in irritation. Of course. I already *knew.* Mrs. Gray had told me the date, but my mind had gone blank. *Now think!* Had she said January or February twenty-eighth? Suddenly, knowing the exact day seemed very important. So much happened in the course of both history and my story between those months. Had the hangings started by then?

Either way, the day I had been in Salem couldn't have been that far into my story — less than halfway. The townspeople would have started to become suspicious, watching for anything unusual to happen. That made sense; it explained why I received so many wary looks.

I squeezed my eyes shut, massaging my forehead to soothe my racing thoughts. I'd written a story, and now, somehow, I had been drawn into it, creating a connection between the past and the present. I had wished for meaningful words and now I had them — words that were so powerful they had blurred the lines between fiction and reality.

Rhetoric

I was only now starting to understand that what I had written had come to life, and the idea spurred excitement in me. But it also incited dread. I wasn't sure if I truly wanted everything I had written to become real.

I finally slipped into bed, peeling back the covers and switching off my lamp. Curled beneath the layers of sheets and blankets, I quickly became warm and drowsy. It didn't take long for me to drop off to sleep.

Slumber

I wasn't usually a light sleeper but tonight, for some reason, I woke up less than an hour later. I couldn't quite pinpoint what had awakened me. Darkness still enveloped me, and I blinked blearily at the ceiling I could just make out overhead. I lay still and listened, but only the fuzzy sound of silence greeted me. Half asleep, I turned over on my side and buried my head beneath my pillow, trying without success to stifle the unrelenting buzz of silence.

Still neither quite asleep nor awake, a now-familiar feeling overtook me. I had just enough time to wonder if what I thought was happening at this moment would actually occur, before a bright flash momentarily lit the room and I was wide awake.

I was once more in Salem in the year 1692, I just knew it. How could this have happened again? The soggy grass beneath the palms of my hands confirmed it. *Great timing for this trip*, I thought, extremely annoyed. *This couldn't be more inconvenient.*

I noticed next that it was no longer nighttime. I scrambled to my feet, all negative thoughts gone. I was eager to get moving and explore this world now, this world that I had somehow created through some wonderful, impossible miracle.

Wonderstruck

I could no longer deny it. This was real. Somehow, I was being drawn into my own story. Not only that, but I also seemed to be pulled into the past. The real 1692. Something had happened that day I had first started writing the story, when all the words came out just right. Somehow, my words had created a connection between my story and the past. As crazy as it sounded, those words were so powerful they had given my fictional world life, merging it with the past. Even if I couldn't comprehend the idea, I had to acknowledge that it could be true.

It wasn't necessarily a good thing. It was amazing, certainly, but it also posed some problems. I'd just traveled here against my will, in the middle of the night. What if it happened again? I didn't particularly like that idea. And what would I do if I traveled to Salem and couldn't get home again?

As a writer, I preferred things to be in their proper places, exactly as they should be. I needed a smooth progression from beginning to end in my writing. But, over the last few days, nothing had been anything close to smooth. This was a whole new world for me.

Reality

As I looked around, I noted the patches of snow

that speckled the land and the almost undetectable change in the air around me. Some amount of time must have passed since I had last been here, but it was impossible to tell just how much I had missed.

I stumbled a few steps and with great relief discovered that I knew where I was. I remembered the grassy fields and houses sprinkled together in clumps. I was on the outskirts of Salem Village, and the Gray family's house wasn't far.

Trudging through the grass and snow and down to the dirt path that served as the road in Salem Village, I reached the Grays' house in only a few minutes. Faith was the person I most wanted to see again. Yes, she played an important role in the story, but I also felt a personal connection to her. She had been so kind and had seemed genuinely nice. Though it had been less than twenty-four hours since we'd met, I was eager to see her again in the flesh, rather than just in my head. It felt like I'd known her for much longer than just a few hours, and I hoped to learn more about her.

I stopped at the doorstep, fully prepared to knock and reintroduce myself if I had to, but for some reason I hesitated and lost my nerve. Faith had seen me evaporate into thin air, for heaven's sake. She must think I'm a demon and probably told her family about my vanishing. They must be horrified, I thought miserably. Now it was unlikely that they would welcome me back into their home. Even before my disappearing act, my behavior must have seemed abnormal and unorthodox to them.

Wondering where I would go instead, I was turning away from the house when a creak sounded from the door behind me. I jumped and spun around, ready to flee.

It was Faith. She looked just as surprised as I did, but after a moment of astonished silence, her face broke into a huge grin. This certainly wasn't what I anticipated. I imagined that she would shrink back in horror and scream, proclaiming for all the neighborhood to hear that I was some horrible fiend.

"It is so wonderful to see you!" Faith lunged forward and wrapped me in a tight hug. I stood stiff and unmoving in my surprise, but eventually I put my arms around her too. Definitely not what I had expected. I was hugging my main character!

Then Faith jumped back quickly, seeming to remember herself. "Heavens, I am terribly sorry. That was most improper of me. I was merely overtaken by my excitement, that is all." Her pale cheeks were flushed, and she eyed me as if she was worried I would be upset.

"No, that's all right," I told her truthfully. "I'm glad you're happy to see me." That was an understatement! I couldn't understand it.

"I cannot quite believe you are back! How were your travels? We were all so disappointed when you had to leave so suddenly."

There was a strange expression on her face that I couldn't interpret. I waited, but she made no mention of just how I had left. She couldn't possibly have missed something as strange as what had happened; she *must* have seen me disappear.

I spied Mrs. Gray behind Faith and, evidently, Faith sensed her presence too. Without moving her head, Faith glanced over her shoulder in the direction of her mother, who moved forward to greet me. "Why, good afternoon, Tess. It is so good to see you. We were disappointed when Faith told us you needed to leave so quickly, without even time for us to bid you farewell. You were gone for so long we quite believed you did not intend to return."

I glanced over at Faith in confusion, and she gave me a small smile. She had covered for me. She hadn't even mentioned my disappearance to her mother. But why not?

"Mother," Faith spoke up, "Might I entertain Tess in my room?" At Mrs. Gray's look of hesitation, Faith hurried on. "I have finished the washing. It is good and proper, I assure you. I feel as though she is my friend already. And Tess is near my age." She turned her attention to me. "Are you not?"

I nodded, knowing how old she was without having to ask. "I'm fifteen."

"My age exactly!" Faith looked back at her mother, who after a moment nodded shortly.

"I suppose there is no harm in it. But only for a short while."

Faith nodded and led me into the house and past her mother. As I passed, I couldn't help but hear Mrs. Gray mutter, "Fifteen — much too young to be traveling alone without a husband."

Faith guided me through the main room and down a short hallway that led to two very small rooms. Faith entered the one on the left. "I share this bedroom with my brother, Will," she explained, when she noticed me looking at the two separate beds.

I'd have thought all of this would have been familiar, but it wasn't. I hadn't ever wondered what Faith's bedroom would be like. This was all new to me.

It was a very simple bedroom, but I liked it nonetheless. Like the rest of the house, the floor was merely wooden boards. There were two mattresses on flimsy-looking wooden bed frames on opposite ends of the crammed room and a single window on one wall. In the middle of the room, a thick green curtain hung from the ceiling to the floor, serving as a divider. On a table in what must have been Faith's side was a basket of needlework. A half-finished piece of fabric hung out. At the foot of William's bed sat a small chest that was open. It was filled with balls, spinning tops, carved wooden soldiers, and other toys.

Faith saw me staring. "Will no longer plays with those toys so often. He is much too old. The other boys would tease him."

I raised my eyebrows. William was only a little kid. "How old is he?"

"Seven."

Faith jumped none too gracefully onto her bed, jostling the headboard and making the whole bed squeak loudly in protest. Her movements seemed freer when she wasn't under the watchful eye of her mother. I perched on the edge of her bed too.

"Mercy, I do believe I have forgotten to tell you my name. I am Faith. There was no time for me to introduce myself when you first came to my family."

I only nodded, not wanting her to know that I already knew her name. My heart fluttered when she said it though, confirming any previous doubts.

"Well?" Faith looked at me in expectance. I only stared back at her. "What really happened that evening nearly two months ago? One moment you were by my side, and the next you were not."

I should have known she would ask me that. "Two months ago? It's been a whole two months?"

"Yes, yes, it is March. Now, what happened? How did you vanish?"

Although it had been less than a day since I had seen her, from Faith's point of view it had been weeks. She must have been waiting for me to return for quite a while, wondering if I would.

"Well, um...you see..." I tried to think of a way to fabricate a story, but I was no good at lying. At that moment, I almost told her the entire truth. That I was from the twenty-first century and that she was part of a story I was writing. That somehow the story had pulled me into its pages and made it possible to travel back and forth between my world and hers. But the words stuck in my mouth and I stopped myself just in time, before I made a terrible mistake.

"Never you mind," Faith was eyeing me strangely. "I have decided I do not really want to know. But there is one thing I have to ask—would you do harm unto this town?"

I furrowed my brows. "What?"

Faith closed her eyes and shook her head vehemently. When she opened them, she spoke again. "What I mean to ask is this: you are no sorceress—no witch?"

I stifled a laugh and tried to look serious. "No, of course I'm not. I promise you, I'm on your side." I hoped I was, anyway.

Faith looked relieved. "Good. Now that that is out of the way, what of your travels?" She watched my face closely. "You have not truly been traveling across the land, have you?"

I shook my head. At least, not the way she thought I was.

Faith's head dropped. "That is too bad. I thought—" She broke off, obviously disappointed.

"But I went to London, once. And California."

Faith's eyes brightened immediately. "In truth? You have been to those faraway lands? I know of London. My grandparents were born there and came here, to the Massachusetts Bay Colony, decades ago. I do not know of this other place, *California*, though. It sounds most exotic. What is it like there?" Her eyes were sparkling, and she looked at me in anticipation.

I realized my mistake immediately. Of course Faith would not know about California. From her point of view it didn't exist yet. It wouldn't become a state for over a century. "It's...well, it's big. Many people live there in, uh, tall buildings with many windows." It was difficult to explain skyscrapers to someone who had never seen them before— especially if she had never heard of cars, trains or modern cities, either.

Faith was much more talkative than I had expected, asking so many questions. I thought she would be more quiet and reserved, and I supposed she was in public, where there were others observing her. She wasn't quite what I had imagined her to be, but I kind of liked that.

"How fascinating!" Faith paused for a moment, and we were both silent. "What is that…unusual costume you wear? I have seen nothing like it."

Glancing down, I winced, realizing I was still in my pajamas. They were bright and flashy, with pink and green polka dots. I would definitely stand out in Salem. It would have been so much more convenient if I hadn't appeared here while I was sleeping. "This is…how we dress where I come from," I said haltingly, not sure how else to explain it.

Faith only raised an eyebrow, a gesture that looked almost comical on someone wearing a modest, full-length Puritan dress. "I see. And do girls wear those blue leggings and tight-fitted attire where you come from as well?"

It took me a moment to realize she was talking about jeans, which I had been wearing last time I saw her. "Um…yes. They are called jeans. They're made of a material called denim."

"Mother noticed your unusual clothing and commented on it after you had left, but she was too courteous to bring the matter to your attention."

Inwardly I groaned. What an impression I had

made on her family! I was surprised they had let me inside their home, considering how out of place and strange I must have looked.

Foreign

"I suppose leggings are very comfortable." Faith wistfully began to fold and weave her fingers together in her lap. "Mother was not keen on them, though. She did say girls ought not wear men's clothing. I rather like them, though."

That made me laugh. "Here." Faith rose and pulled a dress from a peg on the wall. "Mayhap it would be best if you wear one of my dresses. I dare not show you around Salem Village dressed as you are."

"You're going to show me around the village?" That certainly came as a surprise.

"Yes. Indeed I am." Then Faith became shy and meek. "That is, if it pleases you I would be most delighted."

"That'd be great!" I suddenly couldn't wait to spend more time with my character. It was still hard for me to believe I had met her in person. No other writer had done it before—that I knew of, anyway. I wasn't sure how it worked or how it was even possible, but I wished I could talk to Faith about it.

I could just imagine her expression when I told her all about the transportation and exotic places of the twenty-first century, so different from this suppressed

Puritan society. I held out the dress in front of me so I could look at it more closely. Real Puritan clothing, just like I had researched and seen drawings of on the Internet!

The dark blue dress was simple and unadorned, with a stiff, white collar and cuffs. Faith also handed me a cap to match. The skirt nearly brushed the ground when I held the dress up to my shoulders, and the sleeves were long. I imagined it must be a difficult thing to wear in the stifling heat of the coming summer months.

"I thought your mom—I mean your mother—said you had no spare clothing," I commented to Faith.

Faith had been staring at me with a strange expression on her face, but she broke her gaze at the sound of my voice. "Oh? Oh yes, she meant I have but one everyday dress. This is my best dress, the one I wear to church on the Sabbath. Mercy, Mother would have a fit if she knew I let you wear it around the village in the middle of the week, but..." she trailed off, looking unsure of herself.

I doubted she had done something behind her mother's back before. Actually, I knew she hadn't, at least, not this far into her story.

"I do hope it fits you."

I had no worries; I knew it would. I had written Faith to have the same build as me, and she was only slightly shorter than I was. As I slipped the dress over my pajamas, the coarse fabric brushed over my skin in a way that wasn't pleasant. It was fortunate, though, that the dress covered so much of my body that the flashy colors of my pajamas were hidden.

My fingers fumbled with the ties at the back of the dress and Faith reached over to help. Before she could do the final tie at the collar, I pulled away for fear of choking, but Faith shook her head and tied it anyway, the fabric tightening around my neck like a noose. "A girl is not considered dressed if one tie is out of place," she told me, making a face. Something told me she knew this from experience, but I didn't press her for an explanation. I thought I knew everything about Faith by now since I was writing her story, but apparently there were details about her life that I wasn't aware of.

Once I'd pulled on the white cap Faith had given me, we both stepped out of the bedroom and into a short hallway. Faith called out to her mother that she would be back shortly, and she dashed outside with me at her heels before Mrs. Gray could glance up from the large pot she was stirring over the fire. As soon as we got outside, I felt sharp stones on the ground cut into the skin on the soles of my feet, and I couldn't help but cry out.

"You are not wearing shoes!" Faith exclaimed,

stating what I had not realized before. My feet were bare!

In my defense, I had been sleeping moments before I found myself back in Salem Village. But I wished I'd recognized the signs that I was about to fall into my story and grabbed the slippers at the foot of my bed.

Faith bit her lip, looking uncertain. "I fear I can do nothing to remedy the situation. I would lend you some shoes, but these are the only ones I own." She lifted one foot to reveal a battered black boot. "And Mother would surely notice if we borrowed hers."

Gritting my teeth against the pain from the cuts on my feet, I lifted a foot to survey the damage, nearly losing my balance in the long dress. Already, cuts crisscrossed the soles of my feet and the blood slowly seeping from them was mixed with pebbles and flecks of dirt.

"It's all right; I'll manage," I lied, half hoping I would soon return to the present time where Tylenol and antiseptic existed. Who knew what diseases I could catch here?

"If you are certain." Faith shrugged and led me down the path in Salem Village.

"Mrow!" A black cat appeared out of nowhere on a fencepost and leapt to the ground, landing at my feet. I jumped back and tripped on the hem of my dress, grabbing onto Faith's shoulders to keep from falling.

"That is Felicity." Faith leaned down to stroke the mangy cat's dark fur. "She is ours. She came to us about a year ago, and ever since that day she has remained nearby. We feed her whenever we can." She smiled, then something seemed to occur to her and her face hardened. "It is no bad sign, if that is what you assume. I do not believe cats are witches' familiars. They have nothing to do with witchcraft."

"N-no, I wasn't thinking that." I should have known there would be a cat. I had written one into the story just recently, but I hadn't thought about it until now. We started moving through the village again, but a stabbing pain in my feet made me stop in my tracks and bend over to fight the pain.

Shards

Faith stopped and worry filled her eyes. "Mercy, let us return to my house before it becomes worse. My mother can ease the pain. There is no need for me to show you the village right at this moment."

My feet were rubbed raw and the skin was a little shredded, but the bleeding had stopped. "It's not that bad. Let's just stay for a while longer."

Faith sighed. "Very well. But if they begin to bleed again, we must return home at once." She scanned the street, searching for something. Apparently finding what she was looking for a moment later, she dashed away, leaving me to limp after her.

Faith came to a halt next to a small wagon pulled off to the side of the road, and I stopped beside her. A woman sat on the seat of the wagon, rifling through a bag. Though she wore a cap like everyone else, it was black. What stood out most, though, was her dress. It was dyed crimson, the bodice decorated with woven threads of various colors. It was certainly not the usual ensemble for a Puritan woman in the seventeenth century.

"Good day, Goody Sutton," Faith called out, and the woman looked up. When she saw Faith, recognition lit her face.

"Why, Faith Gray! How very good it is to see you. How do you fare this fine day?"

"Very well, I thank you, Goody Sutton." I marveled at Faith's automatic reply and her respectful incline of the head.

The woman turned her attention to me, and her mouth immediately turned downward. "And who might this young lady be?" She directed the question at Faith, who answered quickly.

"Oh, this is my cousin, Te — *Therese*."

The woman's expression softened and Faith spoke again. "Where are you headed?"

"Oh, I have only just returned from Salem Town to gather some supplies for my tavern. Mayhap I will stop at Ingersoll's before I return home."

Faith straightened. "Might we go with you? If it is not a burden, that is. We are seeking a ride there."

"Certainly. You are no burden. Seat yourselves in my wagon and I will give you a ride there in but a moment."

"We are very grateful to you." Faith scrambled into the back of the wagon and I followed. She turned to me. "This is so you will not be required to walk," she explained.

Respite

As the horse pulling the wagon began to move, Faith spoke up again, the rattling of the wagon masking our conversation from anyone in close proximity.

"This is Bridget Sutton, our neighbor. She runs her own tavern here in Salem Village, but many people do consider that improper."

I broke in, perplexed. "Why did you tell her I was your cousin?"

She looked embarrassed. "I am sorry. I know I should not have done such a thing, but, well, Bridget does not take kindly to strangers. No one does. Not anymore. I think it would help if people believe we are kin. Mayhap then they will be more inclined to accept you. Of late, newcomers have not been welcomed in the town. They arouse suspicion." Faith shifted positions in the wagon, spreading her skirts around her.

"Why?"

"What?" Faith looked over, a question in her eyes.

"Why is everyone so suspicious? What is happening?" I knew the reason but wanted to hear Faith's perspective on what was taking place. I held my breath as Faith started to answer.

"Ever since the beginning of the year, things have been odd. Different." She gazed off into the distance, not looking at anything in particular. "Some of the girls in town began to act strange. They would fall down to the floor in fits, screaming that invisible creatures tormented them. They came to meetings bedraggled, and then spoke of how they were tortured during the night."

"By whom?"

Faith met my eyes. "By witches. The girls' fits intensified and became more frequent, until one only had to go to a public place to witness them. The girls would not stop screaming, and they were not able to answer when people begged them to tell who was hurting them.

"At first it was only one girl, Betty Parris. I know her; she lives not far from here. But now more girls fall ill daily, and they have begun to name the witches who cause their afflictions." She let out a shaky breath and met my eyes. "I am afraid, Tess. I fear it won't stop—that these accusations will go on and on until everyone in town has become a witch in the girls' eyes. And after that, there won't be anyone left."

Barren

Faith's chilling prediction made me shudder. She didn't know how close to the truth she was. I ached to tell her what would happen, how the accusations would become trials that would turn into hangings—dozens of gruesome deaths—but what good would those details do her? "Do you think the girls are really being tormented?"

Faith was silent for a moment, but finally she let out a breath and spoke. "I know not. All of it happened so quickly, I can scarcely believe it has actually come to this. Neighbors accusing neighbors. Now everyone is afraid to go outside for too long, whether it is because of their fear of witches or their fear of being accused themselves. We girls have never had any say in our lives. Everything is planned out and chosen for us. No one listens. Mayhap the girls just want somebody to pay attention to them for once in their lives." Faith had a strange look on her face, like she wished she could change things too. That look scared me.

The wagon slowed as we reached a more populated part of the village. People crowded the roads, murmuring to each other in excitement. Faith lowered her voice, but otherwise she didn't seem to notice the crowd.

"All my life, my parents have decided everything for me. As very young children, we learned in school that we must obey our parents. We were made to listen and told we must be obedient. Only speak when we are spoken to, never speak ill of our parents, or anyone. Be respectful of our elders.

"I do not know how the other girls can do it, always docile, the very picture of calmness and sweetness. It is the very thing parents always look for. A single misstep, and one can know for certain that there will be consequences."

Faith was turned away from me, no longer talking to me, but rather simply letting all of her feelings out, because that was what she needed to do. I tried to imagine what she must be feeling, what her life must be like, but I just couldn't. Even though I had written it, I simply couldn't comprehend it. Mom and Dad had always been kind to me, despite the fact that Mom's temper sometimes flared. They let me do what I wanted, and even though they didn't understand my passion for words, they allowed it.

Knowing that I wouldn't be able to quite put myself in Faith's shoes, I tried at least to be a good listener. I could do that much for her.

"I have always wanted to travel," Faith continued. "If I could only see the world beyond my doorstep — but that is unheard of for daughters in a Puritan family,

I quite understand. I will likely stay with my family until they choose a husband for me, and then I will stay in the same, familiar community for the rest of my life. And I will never be able to do or say anything to change that." Faith looked down at the ground, but I caught a glimpse of her tear-filled eyes before she looked away. Although the tears flooded her eyes, she did not cry. I admired her for that.

"Hey," I said softly, resting my hand on her shoulder. "It doesn't have to be like that. Words are powerful. I believe that, and you should too."

Faith looked up at me, doubtful.

"You can change things. *We* will. Don't worry, it won't be like this forever. Someday, we'll get our voice. And I promise I'll stay with you. I'm not going anywhere."

Faith blinked away the tears from her eyes. "Really? Will you not travel on, leaving me here where I will never see you again?"

I looked her in the eyes, completely serious. I would find a way to do this for her. I had to. "No. I'll be here for you. That's what friends are for. I promise."

Chapter Six

Groups of people moved around us, clamoring to reach a building that didn't look nearly large enough to hold the crowd. Bridget Sutton brought the wagon to a stop by the side of the building where other wagons and horses waited. "It is about to start," she called back to us over her shoulder as she jumped down from the wagon. "Mayhap I will stay a bit." Jostling through the crowd, Bridget made her way to the front door of the building and disappeared into the mass of people already inside.

"Oh, it has become out of control." Faith sighed, then tried to mask it as a delicate cough when one of the men nearby gave her a disapproving look. "I daresay the entire village has come, and much of Salem Town as well. One of our neighbors will be questioned in Ingersoll's shortly." She nodded in the direction of the building. "Our meetinghouse. It is Rebecca Nurse. She has been accused of witchcraft. It was a shock for everyone. I can scarcely believe it myself."

The name sounded familiar, as if I had heard it before. I'd probably come across it in my research.

"I cannot believe someone like Rebecca Nurse could possibly be a witch." Faith shook her head, distraught. "It makes no sense. She has always been such a sweet, devout person. I have never known her to speak ill of anyone or miss even one church meeting."

I remained quiet, not knowing what to say. Faith continued on, oblivious to my silence. "People are starting to wonder… At first it seemed possible when neighbors were accused of witchcraft. They were the penniless or impious people, the ones nobody liked. It could have been that they were witches. But now that Rebecca Nurse has been accused, everything has changed. I have heard some people talking, and they have begun to wonder if the afflicted girls really speak in truth."

I watched Faith's expression carefully. "What do you think?"

"I know not what to think." She shrugged. "I know most of the afflicted girls well, and while I do not believe they lie, something just does not seem right."

Wordlessly, we climbed out of the wagon and wove through the crowd, only stopping when we found our way out of it. I spotted a group of girls who stood a little apart from everyone else. Each person that passed greeted them heartily. Hmm. The girls seemed to be something like celebrities. "Who are they?" I turned to Faith, who was observing the girls too.

Faith seemed to startle at the sound of my voice. "Oh, those are the afflicted girls." She began to point them out to me. "Betty Parris, Mary Sutton, Ann Putnam Jr., and Deliverance Johnson. Abigail Williams, Betty's cousin, must be nearby as well. We are certainly lucky no one else has become afflicted yet. Betty and Abigail, the minister's daughter and niece, were the first to fall ill, and the other three fell ill shortly after."

The afflicted girls! I would get to meet them in real life. A flutter of excitement filled me for a moment, which was silly. I still didn't understand how I was being pulled into my story and even through time. Some of these girls were historical figures — I had done my research. Yet I had also made up some of the girls for my story. It was fascinating that the characters that came from my own head mingled here with historical figures.

I was suddenly anxious to meet the girls. From this distance I couldn't see their faces very clearly, so I couldn't make out who was who.

Fortunately, Faith headed toward the girls, so I followed close behind, letting her lead in case I made some kind of mistake in historical etiquette that I knew nothing about. I checked to make sure no flashy colors were showing through the stiff Puritan dress I was wearing. Thankfully, none were.

As we approached, the girls were whispering something to each other and giggling quietly, but then they looked up to notice us. They fastened their eyes on Faith first, and one girl called out, "Well, Faith Gray. What a lovely surprise."

Faith greeted them politely, smiling. "Hello, girls. Hello, Ann." The last part she addressed to the girl who stood in front of the others, who seemed to hold her chin up higher than the rest, as if she had some sort of superiority. I had no doubt she was the ringleader. "It is quite good to see you. I trust you have been feeling well?"

I took a closer look at the ringleader, who must have been Ann Putnam Jr. She didn't look exactly like I thought she would; a few dark strands of hair peeked out from under her loosened cap, and her frame was thin and bony. Then I gasped.

Recognition

Faith and the other girls stopped talking and turned to look at me. I pasted on a smile that probably wasn't very convincing and shrugged at them, and they went back to their conversation after a moment. My mind was whirling faster and faster, like a windmill on a particularly windy day, making you dizzy just watching it. I recognized that girl, and not just because I had written about her, either. She was the one who had rescued me on the streets of Salem the day I had first appeared here.

One thing puzzled me, though. The Ann I had met that day had seemed so friendly. How could this be the same person? I looked at the Ann in front of me once more, but all doubts were erased. The resemblance was too strong. She was the first person I had spoken to here in Salem. Ann Putnam Jr.

She was also the villain in my story.

I hadn't expected Faith's enemy in the story to be so...*nice*. She had seemed pretty likable, if a bit in a hurry, when she had helped me up from the street. She certainly didn't seem like someone who had the capability to — I could barely even think the word — to *kill*.

What had changed? What had made things so different? Maybe my story was no longer exactly how I had written it. But if that was the case, then how had that happened? How was that even possible? How was any of this possible?

I shook my head to clear my thoughts, though it didn't end up being a very successful endeavor. There were just too many questions, and I didn't have any of the right answers.

Inquiries

A blond girl standing at Ann's right side was speaking now, and I forced myself to pay attention. "Yes, I am afraid none of us girls have been feeling well of late." She cocked her head and gave us an exaggerated sad look. "You see, the witches' torments have worsened. One witch in particular will not allow us a moment's rest."

The girl continued on, soaking up the attention she was getting from Faith, who was watching her in awed rapture. My attention was diverted when Ann suddenly cried out and fell to her knees, and my gaze swung over to her instead. I watched in horrified fascination as Ann's limbs began to twitch and the skin on her forearms somehow began to roll and shudder. One of the other girls fell to the ground next to Ann, and another bent over double and clutched at her stomach, biting back a scream.

"Deliverance!" Ann shrieked at the blond girl who was still talking to Faith. "It is her!"

Ann pointed a long, trembling finger across the street, and Faith, Deliverance, and I followed it. A woman stood there looking back at us silently, the men on either side of her clutching her arms to roughly escort her into the meetinghouse. As soon as she saw the woman, Deliverance fell into convulsions and dropped into a fetal position on the ground.

The woman across the street stood there motionless. She was wrinkled and frail, and her hair was almost completely gray. Her dress was a conservative deep gray, and she didn't seem to stand out that much to me. The men at either side of her were trying to pull her along, but she managed to give us an unwavering gaze. I couldn't quite read the expression on her face from this distance, but I thought she looked grim. In shock, I realized this woman was probably Rebecca Nurse, brought here now to be questioned.

When I looked back at the girls, I had trouble looking away. Their fits seemed so *real*. Could they possibly be faking? If this was exactly like my story, I would already know the answer, but in this case I could only guess. The girls were either very good at their games or these afflictions were very, very real.

"Stop it, stop it! She is the one making the needles on my skin!" The smallest girl, who must have been Betty, wailed uncontrollably. All eyes fell on her. A collective gasp rose from the crowd that had turned to watch when Betty held up her arms, which had dozens of pins sticking out of them, piercing her skin. Where had those pins come from? I hadn't noticed them a moment ago.

Betty's scream was bloodcurdling as she yanked

the pins from her skin, and I thought I heard someone in the crowd start sobbing at the sight. Ann tried to get to her feet, stumbling once and nearly falling again. "She does this to us!" she exclaimed. "Can you not see it? We are but playthings to her! She is tormenting us. We are just girls. We never did anything to deserve this!" At this, Ann and the others collapsed, their bodies hitting the ground at the same exact moment.

Unison

Betty heaved one last wracking sob and quieted.

The crowd that had gathered around us rushed forward to comfort the girls while I turned to the street. Rebecca Nurse still stood there, motionless. For one brief moment, her eyes met mine. Then she turned and allowed the men beside her to lead her into the meetinghouse.

Someone gave Ann a hand and pulled her up, and her friends were similarly helped to their feet. Once Ann was standing, she wiped the back of her hand across her brow as if she was wearied. "Such a horrible thing," she moaned. "I do not know how much longer I can stand it. Each time, I expect the torture to get easier, but it never does." She drew out a long breath, then after a moment straightened, assuming the same confident, relaxed position as before. Almost as if nothing had happened.

"Oh, poor child!" A woman with two children

clutching at the folds of her dress pushed through the crowd, closer to Ann and the other girls. "She should not have to put up with such a thing. None of the girls should." The woman gave Ann a look full of sympathy.

Others in the crowd began to speak out too. "Why, just yesterday I spoke with her mother, Ann Putnam Sr. She told me her daughter has fits like these several times a day!"

"How horrible!"

"It is the work of the Devil through his witches. No child should be treated thus. We simply cannot allow it."

"This must be stopped. The witches causing these afflictions can no longer be allowed to do so. They were men and women once, but they signed the Devil's book, and now they have the Devil in them as well. The witches must be put to death!"

The last speaker was a man who stood just behind me. His rough, scratchy voice made me wince, and I turned around so I could see him better. His hair was gray but carefully groomed, and unlike most of the other men in the crowd, he sported a mustache. His black attire was immaculate and contributed to his overall polished look, and he spoke in a quiet but refined way, despite the roughness of his voice. His expression was serious, but calm.

Faith, who was standing beside me but up until

now hadn't even looked over at me, whispered in my ear discreetly. "That is Magistrate John Hathorne. He is the one who will question Rebecca Nurse."

A violent shiver ran down my spine. He seemed like a nice enough man, but he held so much power in this town. I was wary of him. What was going to happen to the town wasn't his fault, but he could have done something to stop it.

Only one group of people was more powerful than the magistrates and public officials in Salem, and that was the group of girls who were standing right in front of me.

Authority

Gradually, the crowd of people around us began to disperse, heading into the meetinghouse to wait for the questioning to begin, until only Faith, Ann's group, and I remained on the street. Faith and I stood mute, neither of us willing to break the silence. Ann and the other girls, however, were not reluctant to speak in the least. "Oh, how I do dread to feel that prickling on my skin!" Betty cried out, but Ann shook her head.

"Hush, Betty, you are the youngest of us, and you must do as we say. No occasion gives you leave to speak out of turn."

Betty hung her head and stared at the hem of her dress, pursing her lips tightly to keep from talking.

I couldn't help but notice a certain part of the

sentence that Ann had uttered. *You must do as we say.* The fierce look on Ann's face told me that while she had said "we," she really meant "I." No one knew what the historical Ann Putnam was like, but this girl in front of me acted much like the way I had imagined she would. Just like the character in my writing that I had based off the historical figure, this girl always had to have everything in control—under *her* control. But now that I saw her in person, I realized just how determined Ann was to manipulate the people around her, regardless of the consequences.

"Why, Faith," Ann was saying now. "You have neglected to introduce us to this friend of yours." She looked at me as if seeing me for the first time. If she recognized me from the day she had saved me, she showed no sign of it. "That is just the tiniest bit rude, do you not think so?" Ann raised her eyebrows, and her companions followed suit, trying to imitate her confidence. Only Betty Parris was still looking at the ground, her brows knit, deep in thought.

Faith flushed visibly. Who was Ann to push her around? Even my solitary self wouldn't allow someone to be that rude to me. Silently, I willed Faith to stand up for herself, but when she spoke, her voice was meek and quiet. I sighed inwardly.

"I am terribly sorry. Forgive me, Ann. I know not what came over me." Faith gestured at me and started to introduce me with a formal air, which she had doubtless learned from her parents and the other adults in town. "Ann Putnam Jr., I present to you my cousin, Therese —"

I startled at the sound of my birth name. Faith had been calling me by that name when she introduced me, which now made sense. Therese probably sounded more like a name that belonged in the seventeenth century, while the name Tess would sound like the name of an outsider. Which, given the circumstances, I technically was.

Suddenly, I realized that Faith had cut off her introduction of me abruptly and was staring back at me in expectation. *Oh.* She wanted to know my last name. "Winters," I said before I could stop myself. "Therese Winters."

Immediately I felt like kicking myself. *Stupid, stupid, stupid.* Why had I given her my real last name? I should have made something up on the spot, but I hadn't thought of it until it was too late. Winters was probably not an ordinary surname for this time.

Ann confirmed my thoughts. "Winters?" I didn't know how it was possible, but somehow her eyebrows rose another inch. "What an...*unusual* name." Her eyes narrowed as she regarded me, and I suddenly feared that she knew everything about me, which was ridiculous. She couldn't know who I was...could she?

Ann's expression told me she didn't especially like me. Either she didn't remember helping me two months ago, or she just didn't care. Maybe in that period of time she had changed to become the heartless girl I saw before me.

Ann and her followers started to leave then, giving me and Faith a formal farewell in parting, although Ann barely deigned to give me a nod. Faith stayed rooted to the spot, so I paused beside her, watching the girls walk away, giggling to each other in exaggerated whispers. Then they paused, and Ann looked over her shoulder at us, and after a moment she headed back over. Mary, Betty, and Deliverance followed her like little chicks. I had a sudden memory, and I nearly gasped aloud at the clarity of it.

I remembered this.

It wasn't that I had experienced it before, because it wasn't quite like a sense of déjà vu. Then it came to me. I had written this. While much of what I had experienced in Salem so far hadn't resembled my story, this particular, simple event had suddenly come to me. I wrote this very scene. I remembered it clearly. Not the moments leading up to it, but just this particular moment itself. And what happened afterward. I knew what Ann was going to say before she even opened her mouth, and my muscles tensed.

Still, I couldn't quite prepare myself for the

moment, no matter how hard I tried. "Faith, after Goody Nurse's examination we will go to Betty and Abigail's house. They promised to show us some rather fascinating magic tricks their servant taught them." The girls around Ann nodded in agreement. "Would you care to join us?" Ann specifically did not look at me, instead directing her attention solely on Faith.

Immediately, Faith's eyes lit up. "Do you speak in truth? I would love—"

A looming dread came over me.

Trepidation

Without stopping to think, I grabbed Faith's arm, clutching it perhaps a bit more tightly than was necessary. "No!" I hissed at her. "You can't go with them."

Faith gave me a perplexed look. "What?" she mouthed, her eyes hardening.

I raised my voice so the other girls could hear too. "Um, what I mean is that Faith and I have other commitments back at her house. We'll be on our way now." I started to tug on Faith's arm, but it was like trying to move a boulder. She was stronger than she seemed.

"Oh, well what a coincidence." Ann stepped in front of me, her voice coated with sugar. The phony sweetness in her voice made me clench my hands, tightening my grip on Faith in the process. Ann continued, "Faith, you nearly pass by the Parris house on your way home. Stay with us for the questioning, and then we can walk to Betty and Abigail's residence together. It will be such fun!"

It didn't escape my notice that Ann had been speaking only to Faith, instead of to both of us. Faith started to say something but I interrupted her in my haste. It was not something I usually did, but I had become desperate. This event was the trigger in the story, the trigger that would launch Faith and the whole town into the path of destruction. I couldn't let that happen.

"No, we really must go now. See you later." With that, I tugged on Faith's arm with all my strength and succeeded in pulling her, protesting, down the road after me.

Behind us, I heard one of the girls speak. " 'See you later'? Is that some kind of vulgar slang? Never before have I heard someone speak in that way."

A voice that was unmistakably Ann's answered, "I cannot understand it, but there is something very unusual about that girl Therese."

Faith and I had moved out of earshot and I could no longer hear what the girls were saying. Using my distraction, Faith pulled her arm from mine, rolling up her sleeve and rubbing her arm where I had clutched it too tightly. I almost apologized at the sight of the deep, crescent-shaped indentations on her bare skin, but Faith spoke first. Her voice held an anger that I had not heard coming from her before.

"Whatever possessed you to act in this way? Could you not see that I wished to go with them?" Her expression was fierce, and I couldn't help but shrink back just a little with all this anger directed at me. "Did you not see that they could be my friends? It has been years since they have spoken more than a passing greeting to me, and now, when they finally give me a chance to be a part of their circle you take it away from me." Faith turned quiet now, and her rage gave way to dejection. She wouldn't look at me. She began walking faster, and I hurried to catch up.

I was at a loss for words. Finally, I opened my mouth. "Faith—Faith, I'm so sorry. I know how much being a part of that group means to you, but you just have to trust me on this. Can you do that—can you please just try to trust me?"

I sighed heavily in frustration, wanting to reveal more, but what else could I say? I couldn't explain how I knew that a friendship with Ann and the other girls would not end well. It was probably best to let Faith think that I was merely following my instincts.

We walked in the direction of Salem Village in stony silence. The cuts on the soles of my feet had reopened, and as I walked I left behind pink streaks in the patches of snow. I kept glancing over at Faith, but she refused to look at me, instead staring intently forward.

As we walked, the inevitable thoughts of home came to me. I had been here for a long time today, much longer than my last visit. I didn't know how much time had passed, but it must have been hours. Suddenly, a longing to be back home with my family overwhelmed me. Here I was, stuck in my own story—and in 1692—and I no longer had any control over either one.

Futile

A startling thought came to me then. My time here had lasted too long. What if the force that had made it possible to live my own story also made it impossible for me to return to my real life? What would I do if I could no longer go back?

My breath hitched and unbidden tears came to my eyes. I tried to reassure myself silently. I had done it once before. I had "flashed"—as I had come to think of it—into my story and returned to real life again, unharmed for the most part. I tried to remember the events of my return as clearly as I could. Had it truly only been a day since I discovered that such a thing was even physically possible? The one image that refused to leave my mind was the shocked—no, terrified—look on Faith's face as I disappeared right before her eyes.

I tried to recall how I had felt just before that moment. Dizzy and nauseous, I supposed, just like the two times I'd traveled here. Having that indicator was something of a relief to me, and I let out the breath that I hadn't realized I'd been holding. At least I now had some signal before appearing into or disappearing out of my story, so I wouldn't be completely unprepared. Maybe I could prevent other people from witnessing what happened to me next time, though if they did notice, they most likely wouldn't believe their eyes.

Next time. It scared me how my thoughts had changed in such a short amount of time. How I now expected there to *be* a next time. Would it always be this way for me, flashing back and forth between reality and fiction? What if my story never ended, and eventually my life just melded with my story? Would I forever be a part of the historical time that was the setting for my story? I would become my story, and it would be me, always.

Shackled

My words would be inescapable, though I had written them to become free. It was a horribly ironic thought.

I stopped in the middle of the dirt road, not caring that Faith was watching. Picking up a forked stick lying off the path in a thick patch of grass, I turned it over in my hands a few times and crouched down, dragging the stick through the dirt.

By this time, Faith had noticed I'd stopped walking and she stood a few feet away, a bewildered look on her face. I ignored her.

I finished scratching out the first word.

Ironic

After I had formed the letters in the dirt, I stared at them for a few moments, merely contemplating them. Then, beneath it, I wrote two more words:

What if

"What ifs" had begun to take control of my life lately — what if things never changed? What if they did? What if I would never be the writer I wanted to be? What if I never met a person who truly understood me?

What if my words were never quite right?

Finally, after much hesitation, I added another word beneath the ones I had already written in the dirt at my feet.

Forever

Because that was what I was most afraid of.

Clumsily, I got to my feet, avoiding Faith's inquiring gaze. I stared down at the words I had written on the ground. They were so tiny when I looked at them this way. So insignificant. I stamped one foot down on the words hard, grinding the dirt with my heel. When I lifted my foot, the words were smudged and blurred, but they hadn't disappeared.

It wasn't that easy.

Chapter Seven

Faith seemed to have forgotten all about her anger toward me for keeping her away from Ann Putnam and the others. On the way back to her house, she asked me more about my supposed travels, and I dodged her questions reluctantly, careful not to give her a direct answer or reveal too much. I did describe the time when I was eight that my parents and I had traveled to London to see an art exhibition that Dad had been raving about for months. Faith had gasped at my estimate of the number of people all in one place and my descriptions of the five-star hotel we had stayed in for two nights.

By the time we returned to her house, Faith was relaxed and chatting contentedly. "And I am certain Mother will allow you to stay with us for the night.

There are no" — Faith scrunched up her face — "*hotels*, as you call them, in Salem Town because we rarely entertain new visitors, but surely Mother and Father will not mind. I do not think that the witch examinations happening now will deter them. I know not if they are skeptical about this whole witch business, but they try to stay out of it. My family prefers the solitude of the village, and we do not go to town so often. We stay to ourselves more than other families do."

That was news to me. I wondered what else I didn't know about this family. I hadn't spent all that much time developing the Grays in my writing, and very few of my scenes actually featured any of them. Except Faith, of course. She was the heroine of the story, although I was beginning to discover that what I thought I knew about her before wasn't true anymore.

Faith's voice brought me back to the present. "It will be such fun! I am certain you may sleep in my room, and we can arrange bedding for you. William will not mind an extra person in the bedroom — he will find it exciting. Ever since you left, I have, well…I have missed you."

The raw honesty of Faith's words struck my heart, and I smiled softly. "I missed you too." I realized it was true, though I had seen her only yesterday. It dawned on me that I enjoyed being around Faith, with all of her merits and faults. I hadn't imagined that this place would be so unpredictable. Faith was like that too. I almost laughed to myself. One of my new best friends was somehow a fictional character that I had invented myself.

Faith started to speak again, and her voice cracked. "You…you *are* going to stay for the night, are you not? You are not planning to…" She paused, trying to find the right words. We both knew what she meant. "You will not leave, will you?"

I gave her a pained smile at the hopefulness etched on her face, and I assured her, like I had before, that I wasn't planning to.

Faith and I had just walked in through the door when Mrs. Gray hurried up to us. "Oh, good, you have returned." She turned us around and marched us straight outside, not listening to Faith's protests. We reached the back of the house where a large black kettle sat on the patchy, water-starved grass. "I could use some help making soap, girls."

Faith looked annoyed. "Mother, Tess is our guest, is she not? Do you not think it would be best for us to make the soap by ourselves? Surely we can manage."

Mrs. Gray shook her head. "We need all the help we can get. This job is too big for only two people. And Tess would not mind working a bit during her stay." She looked at me, daring me to defy her. "Would you?"

"Oh, of course not ma'am," I said quickly, remembering too late that seventeenth century Puritans didn't say ma'am. Fortunately, no one seemed to notice or care.

From where we stood I had a good view of the dirt road. I happened to be looking in that direction when a woman passing by stopped, glancing in our direction. "I wish you luck with your soap, Charity!" she called out from the road.

Mrs. Gray looked up from where she stood by the black kettle. "Oh, I thank you. We hope for the best."

I turned to Faith. "What does she mean?"

"Oh, have you not made soap before? It takes much time, and sometimes it does not work. No one knows why."

With that promising thought, we began the process. Mrs. Gray poured a container of some liquid into the kettle and had Faith bring her a bucket of water, which she added to the kettle as well. When Faith returned to my side, she explained, "We already made the wood ash lye yesterday, and now we must render the cooking grease." When she saw that I didn't understand anything that she was saying, she clarified. "Clean it, rid it of impurities. We have been saving the extra grease for months to have enough to make the soap."

Mrs. Gray started a fire, and Faith and I hoisted

the kettle over the open flame. I couldn't help but wrinkle my nose at the rancid smell that arose from the grease. Faith was also having trouble refraining from covering her nose. The air around us grew foul. It was a good thing we were doing this outdoors.

It took a great deal of time for the mixture to boil, but once Mrs. Gray was satisfied with its appearance, she called for more water and put out the fire. She poured the rest of the water into the kettle. "There."

"So are we done?" I was barely able to endure the stench from the reeking pot.

Both Faith and her mother laughed. "Oh, no," Mrs. Gray answered. "The most difficult part is yet to come. We must combine the wood ash lye and grease to make the actual soap. That will not be until tomorrow, though. The mixture must cool overnight."

The soap-making had taken so long that we didn't eat anything until darkness had fallen. We ate at the table quickly, and this time I remembered to stand as I ate. I hoped I didn't make as many mistakes as I had at my last meal with the Gray family.

In any case, Faith's parents took no notice. They spent the meal talking to each other in tense voices about news that a neighbor had given them of Rebecca Nurse's examination. They fervently hoped that she would be found innocent and were shocked that such a pious, devout woman could possibly be a witch.

I hated that I knew the truth, and I wished it didn't have to be this way: Rebecca Nurse would not survive another four months.

Throughout the course of the light meal, the only time Mrs. Gray spoke to me was to apologize that this time there was no meat because they had run out of salt to preserve it, and their remaining bits had spoiled. I could not help but be a little relieved that I wouldn't have to choke down venison or some other strange meat.

William and Faith were dismissed from the table fairly early, and although their parents invited me to stay a bit longer because I was a guest, I declined as politely as I could. Not an hour later, Faith and I lay in the darkness under a thin blanket on her bed. I hadn't noticed before how dark it was here. Without the street lights or the hundreds of colorful dots of a city in the distance, it seemed so empty and quiet. As I stared at the invisible ceiling above me, Faith's voice came from the darkness.

"Mother would not like your sharing the bed with me, but of course I do not mind. I could not bear forcing you to sleep on the floor, anyhow. The rats would devour you whole."

There were rats? I curled up even tighter beneath the scratchy blanket that gave me no warmth and pressed my head against the undecorated headboard of the bed. Next to me, Faith tried to muffle a laugh.

Then we were quiet. How silent it was — the only sound to be heard was the stridulating of the crickets outside. No sounds of traffic or whirring of a heating system, or even a plane passing by overhead.

Serenity

It was refreshing. This was one of the first times since I had first come here that I actually liked this place. It was so peaceful at night. It was almost like the many strict rules didn't apply as much at night. They could be bent.

Faith had not spoken for so long that I assumed she had fallen asleep. But she hadn't. She sat up quickly, turning to me. "Would it not be a wonderful time to visit the Parris household?" She had already scrambled out of bed and was twisting and pinning her loose hair to her head.

In alarm, I sat up in bed too. "Are you crazy?" Apparently I wasn't alone in thinking that night was a good time to break rules.

Faith stopped what she was doing to give me a funny look. "Whatever do you mean? I am perfectly sane." She paused. "I only thought it would be fun. A sort of adventure, if you take my meaning." Even in the dark I could see her eyes sparkle.

Mischief

I shouldn't have caved to her, but deep down I knew I couldn't stop her. "Okay." If Faith wanted to see the tricks Betty and Abigail had learned from their servant, I'd just have to come with her. With any luck, Ann and the other girls wouldn't be there. The entire household would most likely be asleep at this time of night, anyway.

To assuage my guilt, I told myself that it could be a good experience for Faith too. If what I thought was true, she didn't know much about witchcraft, or witches at all. This could help her, make her understand. Maybe it could even change a decision she would make in the future and ultimately alter the story. After all, the ending hadn't been written yet.

Possibilities

"Ready!" Faith had finished securing her hair, and with haste she tucked it beneath a cap. She handed me the cap I had hung back on the peg after supper, and I pulled my hair up underneath it.

Faith looked about ready to dash out the door of the bedroom. "Wait!" I called out in an exaggerated whisper. "Are you really going to go out wearing that?" I gestured to the plain white nightgown she was wearing. I had slept in the same rumpled dress Faith had given me earlier. She only had one nightgown, and I was reluctant to sleep in my modern pajamas, which I still wore underneath my Puritan dress.

Faith looked down at her dress and shrugged. At least, that's what it looked like she was doing. In the darkness, all I could really see was her form. "The girls will not mind. And no one else will see us."

For your sake, I hope you're right. When Faith gave me a strange look, I realized I had spoken that thought aloud, and I bit my lip hard enough to make it bleed. Words were supposed to be my specialty. Why couldn't I say anything right?

Burden

When I looked over at Faith, she was already creeping out of the bedroom and into the main part of the house.

She gave me no choice but to follow her, but I glanced back in the direction of William's side of the room. "Shh!" I knew without asking that Faith wasn't particularly experienced in stealth.

Faith looked back at me askance and then noticed where I was looking. "Oh, do not fear, Tess. Will is such a sound sleeper. He sleeps like a log. And Mother and Father will not wake, either."

We made it out of the house safely, although I jumped about a foot in the air when Faith opened the front door and it creaked loudly. I wasn't too practiced in sneaking out of houses in the dead of night, either.

We walked just enough to get out of sight of the Grays' home and then stopped. I shifted from one leg to the other, crossing my arms over my chest to ward off the cold. My eyes shifted back and forth too, automatically searching for figures darting from shadow to shadow.

"Okay. So where is the Parris house?"

Faith's eyes darted in all directions as mine were doing, but she seemed to be looking around in calculated composure. Trying to get a sense of direction, I discovered, after a few moments of silence. It was harder to tell where we were at night, and I could only hope that Faith knew the way through Salem Village with her eyes closed.

"Not far. Just past the heart of Salem Village."

My heart sank. How were we to remain unnoticed there? Surely there would be people out in that area, even at this time of night. But no girls. Anyone who saw two girls lurking in the shadows in the dead of night would be suspicious. I just hoped we would not draw any unwanted attention.

"Halt! Who goes there? If you be the Devil, you are not welcome here!"

My breath and Faith's both hitched in unison. I scanned the area around us, and at first I didn't notice the woman folded into the shadows of a building. Her bright red dress seemed to glow in the darkness and I could just make out the rest of her profile.

Silhouette

Faith backed away a few steps. "It is our neighbor, Bridget Sutton!" she hissed at me.

She was staring straight at us. There was no doubt about that. I backed away too, my heart beating rapidly in my chest. "Run!" I yelled at Faith, and we both turned on our heels and raced in the opposite direction.

"Wait!" Goody Sutton called after us. "You cannot get away unseen. I shall report this to the constable!"

Repercussions

Faith and I didn't stop to look back. We raced down the street, our feet kicking up dirt and snow. At that moment, I didn't care how much sound we were making or who else saw us. This was a bad idea, I just knew it was. But it was too late to return to the Grays' house. For all I knew, they may have already awakened and realized that Faith and I were no longer there. My only thought was of keeping Faith safe.

I grabbed Faith by the hand and together we ran. I was glad Mrs. Gray had bound my feet in cloth earlier, so it didn't hurt as much to run. Our breathing was labored, and I tripped and stumbled over the hem of my skirt, which had collected dirt and was wet from the snow on the road.

Shouts echoed behind us, but they came from far off. For now, we were outrunning whoever was chasing us.

A thought came to me then, in the midst of the chaos and panic. Why should I care? Why should I care about Faith and her family, or any of them? They were not real. All of this had just been created by my overactive imagination. And even though my story seemed to have brought my characters to life, shoving me into a world where the past and my story were connected, 1692 was centuries ago. If all of this had already happened, and all of these people were dead and gone long before the twenty-first century, none of this should feel real to me, should it?

This was fiction. I shouldn't care.

And yet, for some reason, I did. I cared very much. Maybe it was because I had gotten a glimpse of their lives. I felt that even though I may have created her, Faith wasn't so different from me after all. And now she was my friend. I wasn't about to let Faith get arrested.

Finally, we stopped to catch our breath. "Have we gone the right way?" I had lost all sense of direction.

Astray

Faith let herself fall against the side of a building, one that was similar to her house, but better built. She gasped for breath, struggling to speak for several moments. Then I recognized where we were. Without realizing it, we had run all the way to the center of Salem Village. Even in the darkness I remembered our surroundings. We were not far from the meetinghouse we had gone to earlier today.

"Yes." Faith looked around, blinking several times to clear her vision. "I made sure of that. This is the Parris house."

She had made sure of that? She had been beside me most of the time, and I had merely run blindly through the streets, not minding where I was going at all. If Faith was able to navigate through the village in the darkness with people pursuing us, then she was much more composed and collected in the face of disaster than I was.

That could come in handy.

Faith just stared at the ground, not moving in the direction of the Parris house. She pressed her hand to her side and tried to hide a grimace.

"What is it?" I exclaimed. "Are you hurt?"

Faith didn't answer. I managed to gently pry her hand from her side. A dark liquid stained the side of her nightgown, standing out grotesquely against the white fabric. I stifled a gasp. It was blood.

Plight

"It is not as bad as it looks." Faith's voice was strained.

"It looks bad enough! How on earth did it happen? Here, let me help you sit down." I put my arm around her and started to help her sit in the dirt on the ground, but Faith just shook me off.

"I shall be fine in a moment, I think. But I know the cause. This was a witch's doing. Our neighbor is a witch—there can be no other explanation for this infliction."

I was doubtful. I could think of a few explanations more likely than the one Faith had proposed. Maybe she had bumped into something sharp as we fled. "First things first," I told her, taking charge of the situation. "We need to get you cleaned up." I pulled the cap from my head and handed it to her. She pressed it to her side to staunch the flow. After a few moments of terse silence, Faith gingerly lifted it away and wiped at her nightdress and fingers, which were darkened with blood. The flow seemed to have stopped, and the only sign that remained was the ruined cap and the rust-colored stain on the white fabric of her nightgown.

"I really am fine," Faith told me again. "It was not really that much blood, and the cut has already closed. It was no more than the span of a fingernail, anyway."

What she said didn't particularly reassure me. "Where is the doctor? We should go to him, just to be safe."

"No doctor. Besides, how would we explain ourselves? We were merely taking a midnight stroll through the village?" Faith raised her eyebrows, and I wished she would step into a patch of light so I could better assess her condition. "Let us go inside the Parris house as we planned. Their servant, Tituba, keeps all kinds of medicines and tonics if need be."

I was reluctant to agree, but eventually I gave in. "Come, let us make haste." Faith rushed to the door, completely forgetting about her injury in her excitement.

I raced to catch up with Faith and stopped beside her at the front door. A lantern shone through the front window. We weren't the only ones awake. "Well, aren't we going to go in?" I asked, not wanting to be the one to knock on the door.

"Oh yes, of course." Faith apparently was not inclined to be the first to announce our presence either, but she reached up and rapped on the thick wooden door three times, decisively.

Within moments, the door opened, and I flinched involuntarily at the sudden noise. A small girl peeked out at us. It was Betty Parris. "Oh, hello Faith." Her eyes flickered to me. "Therese. I suppose you have come to see the tricks, just like the others."

The others? Faith and I exchanged a glance, and Betty moved aside. Behind her was a small group of girls gathered in a circle. In the center stood Ann Putnam, who locked eyes with me and smirked.

Chapter Eight

"Well, what a pleasure it is to see you two girls here on this fine night." Ann's voice was overly sweet.

Saccharine

Ann and the other girls eyed Faith with interest. "I did not expect you would change your mind and join us in our fun, Faith," Ann commented dryly. "It is a pleasure. Although..." Ann paused to shoot me a look of distaste. "Mayhap you should not have dragged along your little cousin. Ah, but it is for the best. We shall be a merry group, we nine." I noticed then that two more girls had joined the group since we had last seen Ann. I didn't recognize either of them.

Just then Faith spoke up. "Why are you here, Ann? You told us you would visit, but that was hours ago. Surely you have not passed all that time here."

Ann laughed. "Of course not, addled-brain. We only decided it is more fitting to attempt this at night."

Before I could lunge at her in anger—how could I have ever liked this girl?—one of the girls broke in timidly. "Ann, do you not think that you ought to keep your tongue in check? Mayhap your words are too harsh." I guessed that the speaker was Mary Sutton, one of the girls Faith had pointed out at the meetinghouse.

Ann spun on her, anger flashing in her eyes. "Might I remind you, Mary, that you are but a *tavern wench*." She stomped her foot on the floor in emphasis. "My father is Thomas Putnam, and my mother is Ann Putnam Sr. I am of high rank in Salem, and a person such as yourself should not speak to me thus!"

Mary only nodded meekly and stepped back. Just then, the blond girl, Deliverance, cried out. I turned to her, half-expecting her to fall into a fit like the others had earlier today in town. But instead, she pointed at Faith. "Heavens! Faith, what has befallen you?"

Everyone seemed to notice the blood on Faith's nightgown at once. "It is the work of the Devil!" Ann cried out. The girls in the room gave a collective gasp and all began talking at once.

"Do you have any bandages?" I asked, trying to catch Betty's attention. "Faith's cut needs to be treated.

Can't you do anything for her?" Even though the gash was small, it could still get infected.

Betty shrugged. "I suppose I could tear some cloth for bandages if she wished me to do so, but…"

"No!" Faith had been watching us, and now she began to protest. "I mean, as I have said, it is a mere scratch. It only looks ever so much worse."

Ann nodded. "That is the way of the Devil. He is cunning. The wounds are meant to bring pain to the eyes of the observers rather than to the body of the person harmed. But then the tides do turn. As we know all too well, do we not, girls?" Ann turned to the rest of her group, and they all nodded simultaneously.

"It is a horror," Deliverance cried out. "More and more witches are showing themselves in this town. They torment us increasingly each day. And now ill has befallen our beloved Faith. It is without a doubt that the witches have begun to torment her as well!"

The other girls nodded in agreement and put on expressions of sadness, though I thought I could see through them to their true gleefulness at having someone join their group as an afflicted girl.

Suddenly it was too much. It disgusted me. I threw my hands up in exasperation. "There are no such things as witches!" I yelled, my voice filling the room.

Everyone fell silent. Suddenly, all eyes were on me. I ducked my head, trying to avoid eye contact.

That exclamation had not been a smart move. I knew that for certain even before Ann opened her mouth to speak. "And how can you possibly be so sure of that, dear? As far as we know, you could be in league with the very witches you claim do not exist." Ann's tone was casual, but her eyes were hard.

"Hush." Betty stood still, listening. "We must not allow my parents to hear us. They are asleep."

Everyone paused to listen, but I heard nothing. Miraculously, Betty's parents had slept through my shouting.

"Let us try the trick that our servant, Tituba, taught us." The girls gathered around a table in the middle of the room, but I hung back.

As Mary passed me, she stopped and turned. "Do not heed Ann's words so much. I have known her for years, and she never used to be this way. She has gotten herself caught up in the uncovering of witches, and it has changed her." She paused to look over at Faith. "And as for Faith, I think she is right. Her cut is not nearly as bad as it seems." She turned to join the group at the table, and I watched her go.

Betty was talking now, gesturing at a glass on the table. "Tituba taught us this trick just before she was jailed for witchcraft. It is magic, to be sure."

"But not black magic, surely? It is harmless, is it not?"

"Of course. See, just place the egg white in the water, and it will show you the face of the man you will marry."

I glanced over at Faith, who was squeezed in between Deliverance and Ann, looking intently into the bowl that held the egg white. I could hardly conceal my frustration and annoyance. This was a waste of time, coming here. Especially with Ann and the other girls here as well. It would probably do more harm than good, in fact.

Faith was surrounded by the other girls, laughing at something Deliverance had just said. I hated to admit it, but at that moment, it looked like she belonged with them. Not with me. What kind of company was I, anyway? I hadn't even been entirely truthful with Faith, and I knew that I never could be the friend to her that I would have liked to be.

Faith looked up at me then, not seeming to notice my distress. Her eyes shone. "You should come over here and see, Tess!" she said, in her excitement forgetting to call me Therese.

I shook my head. "That's all right; I'll take my turn later." It was a lie, but no one was paying attention.

Faith's health seemed to have improved since we had entered the Parris house. Her wound really didn't seem that bad now. It was just a minor cut.

The darkness outside must have made it seem worse than it really was.

I sat in one of the two wooden chairs in the corner of the room and watched the girls, letting Faith enjoy herself. She deserved that much, anyway, after everything that she had gone through already.

Without warning, cries arose from the center of the room, and I jerked my head up. "That is not the shape of a face," Betty whispered. "That is the shape of a coffin."

Premonition

A sharp lurch in my stomach caught me off guard, but it had nothing to do with the bad omen. My vision swam, and I began to feel the pounding pain that would soon reach my eyes.

Oh no. Of all places, why here? I knew what this feeling meant. "Uh, Faith," I called out, watching the blurred figures of the girls at the table. "Would you care for a quick walk outside?" Faith looked up and stared at me for a moment. I must have looked terrible, because her eyes widened, and she got up and excused herself from the other girls right away.

I stood, trying but failing to ignore the overwhelming dizziness. Why didn't this ever get any easier? One of the girls—I thought it was Ann—looked up and noticed Faith and I were leaving. "Girls, why do you leave in such a hurry? Where are you going?"

I managed to make it to the door and pull it open, stepping out into the night. My vision was already becoming blurrier, and I could barely stand on my own. It would happen soon—any moment now. Faith grabbed my arm to steady me, and we rushed around the house to the back. I hoped desperately that none of the girls would become curious and follow us. Thankfully, there weren't any windows in the back of the house, so they couldn't peer out and watch us.

"It is happening again, is it not?" I could distinguish Faith's somber tone, even though I could no longer make out her face clearly.

I nodded and sat down on a large rock that jutted out from the ground. Faith crouched beside me and rubbed my back, talking to me in low, soothing tones, although I knew she must be as scared as I was. "There, there. It is all right."

"Faith? Therese? Where have you gone?"

It was Ann's voice, calling to us from the front of the house, only a few dozen yards from where we sat. I tensed, and my forehead exploded in pain.

"Do not worry; she will not spot us in the shadows." Even as Faith spoke, though, her hand tightened around mine.

"Therese? Faith?" Ann's voice was close. Too close. I squeezed my eyes shut. Any time now.

Imminent

"Faith," I risked whispering into the darkness.

"Yes?"

"I will come back. I won't stop trying until I can. Don't worry. We will see each other again."

Then Faith's hand slipped from mine. I thought at first that she had let go of me, but in actuality, there was no longer anything for her to hold on to.

Chapter Nine

The sudden light forced me to blink several times before I was able to see anything more than blinding white.

Flash

It was fortunate that I had found myself in my room again and not in the path of an oncoming school bus or the like. I scrambled to my feet, glad that the effects of the dizziness did not remain.

Glancing at my clock, I discovered it was midday, which made no sense, but I was beginning to accept that fact. How many hours had passed? It had been nighttime when I had flashed into the story, so now it was probably the next day.

Once my scramble of thoughts had more or less cleared, I noticed that my door had been left ajar.

Strange. I was sure I had closed it when I went to bed the night before.

That should have been the first thing that told me something was wrong. But I didn't realize it until I went downstairs and found Mom on the couch of the living room, talking frantically into the phone pressed to her ear.

"You're telling me you haven't found anything? Please, I'm begging you, please find her. Have you checked the park? That should have been the first place to look."

There were deep circles beneath her eyes, and her hair was matted and hadn't been styled recently. Fatigue filled her face, and she looked as if she had not rested in a long time.

I padded hesitantly into the room, lingering near the hallway, and at the sound of my feet on the carpet Mom looked up and her eyes met mine.

Mom shrieked and dropped the phone, which clattered to the ground unnoticed. "Tess!" She stood and ran over to me, folding me into her arms. I hugged her back tentatively. "We thought you were gone! When I couldn't find you, I thought— We called the police and filed a report, and they've been searching— Oh, baby, are you all right?"

Oh no. She must have noticed I was no longer here when I disappeared into my story at night. And more time must have passed than I had thought. "I'm fine Mom. But…what day is it?" I had to know how much time had passed.

"Tuesday," Mom sobbed. "You've been missing for more than two days."

In shock, I could only stare back at her tearstained face. She was right. I had flashed into Salem on Saturday night, and now it was Tuesday. A sudden thought occurred to me. "Where's Dad?"

"He's in the city looking for you. We've been searching everywhere, but I thought it best to stay home in case you came back. Oh, dear me," Mom went over to the couch and picked up the phone she had dropped, placing it to her ear for a moment. Evidently, the person she had been speaking to had hung up, because after a moment she did so as well.

When Mom turned to me, she seemed a bit more collected. More like herself. "Now, young lady, where have you been? I've been worried sick, and Ms. Wilson had to take over for me at work. Where have you been?"

I was in deep trouble. How was I going to explain this? There was no easy way to work around the fact that I had been missing from this world for two whole days. "I, uh, I was at a friend's house." It was not entirely a lie. "I would have called you, but I forgot my phone, and she doesn't have one." It was a pathetic excuse — I knew it and so did my mother.

"Hazel? But we called her and she said she hadn't heard from you in days."

At the mention of Hazel, a twinge of guilt twisted in my stomach. She must have left me dozens of messages on my phone, which was probably sitting on my table in my room, turned off like always. "No, it's someone else. I just met her a while ago." I stumbled over my words, trying to give her a plausible explanation. If I told her that I had been sucked into a story that had brought history to life and had spent the past two days there, she would send me to a psychiatrist. Or to a mental institution.

Mom narrowed her eyes, but then seemed to look at me closely for the first time. "What on earth are you wearing?"

I looked down. Great, I still wore Faith's dress. At least I no longer had the blood-soaked cap. That would really alarm Mom.

I thought about it for a moment. I had come back wearing Faith's dress, just as I had returned with melted snow on my clothes the first time.

My words were even more powerful than I had thought. I could bring things back and forth with me, like Faith's dress. Yet more proof that this world was real, that the power of my words truly had made it possible for me to interact with my characters and experience life in 1692. Another thought occurred to me. Did that mean I also had the ability to rewrite history? There was still so much about the connection between my story and history that I didn't understand.

Mom's impatient look told me that I had no more time to dwell on the matter. "We were, uh…that is, we went to a costume party."

Lies

"But I promise I won't go out ever again without your permission. It was wrong of me, I know." I attempted to mend my statement.

"You bet it was. You can't possibly imagine how scared I was that something had happened." Mom's face softened. "Why don't you go upstairs and rest for a while. You must be exhausted. We'll talk more about this later, when your father comes home. I'd better go call him back now."

I couldn't believe how easily she was letting me off, but I knew my luck wouldn't last long when they started to demand real answers.

Back in my room, I reached for my phone and turned it on to check my messages. I needed to distract myself from thinking about Faith and what had happened after I had left.

My phone in my hand began to beep loudly, one beep for every message I had missed. I yelped, nearly dropping my phone at the sudden noise. It continued to beep persistently for another minute. Had it broken? Finally, it fell silent and I stared at the screen. My eyes bugged out. Fourteen voice messages and forty-two texts. I didn't check my phone often, but several days ago I had charged it and checked the few missed messages that I had received.

I scrolled through the first few texts, which started Saturday, the first day that I had flashed into my story, and went through today. All of them were from Hazel. I scanned over a few of them:

"Still coming to meet my friends tomorrow? You'd better. It'll be fun!"

"Where R U?"

"Call me back when U get this."

"OK, I'm really starting to freak out now. Your parents just called me. Where are U, girl??"

"TESS?!?"

I sighed. I didn't really want to check my voicemail anymore. Guilt ebbed its way deeper inside me. I needed to call Hazel back and tell her I was okay.

Just then, loud pop music that Hazel had chosen for my ringtone burst from the speaker of my phone. I pressed talk and held it to my ear. "Hello?"

"Tess? Oh my gosh, it's you! You really answered. I can't believe it. Are you okay? Where are you? What happened? Why did your mom call me? Did you run away? You know, you totally blew us off at the coffee shop the other day. We were all so disappointed!" Hazel spoke so fast it was difficult to distinguish one word from the next.

"Hazel, I'm so sorry I didn't come meet your friends. Mom had me grounded that day." It was technically true, but I had been inside my story, three centuries earlier, interacting with my characters when I was supposed to meet Hazel. "And…well, everything else is just really complicated. I can't explain it any better than that, trust me."

I heard Hazel make a *hmph* sound into the phone. "Sounds like things are seriously messed up in your life right now."

I couldn't help but laugh. She didn't know the half of it.

"Listen," Hazel continued, "How about if you and I hang out for a while? There's this cool place I found not far from my house. You'd really like it. There's a little waterfall and rocks, and it looks like it's out in the middle of nowhere, except it's not. And you can watch the sun set from there. It's far enough away from the city lights that you can even see the stars at night too. Real inspiration-y. I thought maybe we could go there together and it might help with your writer's block. You know, you've been telling me lately how you don't know what to write about. Well, maybe this might help."

I sighed. "Hazel…"

"I was going to surprise you and take you there after you met my friends, but you didn't show up, so I didn't get the chance. But now would be the perfect time. It's not dark yet, so at least you'll get to see the waterfall."

I sat at my desk and rested my head on my hand. She had planned a surprise for me. I remembered the night we had bumped into each other in the city when I was leaving the park. She had acted so restless and nervous, and now I knew why. She had probably discovered that spot, and was already planning to surprise me with it sometime, knowing how much I loved nature.

What kind of friend had I been lately? I hadn't spoken with Hazel in days, even though I'd had the opportunity to several times.

Mistakes

I couldn't be entirely truthful with her or with anybody—not even Faith. "Could we do it some other time? I don't really feel up to it now."

"Sure! Whatever you say, girl!" Hazel sounded perky and quick to agree, but I still caught the disappointment in her voice.

"I-I just need some time to figure all this out. When everything is back to normal, we'll go to that place you found and spend all day together and get drenched in that waterfall, okay?"

Hazel's voice seemed to brighten. "Okay!" She hung up without saying goodbye, which was characteristic of her.

Setting my phone aside, I turned to my writing notebook, which was once again lying open, though I had closed it after I had last used it. I reached for my gold pen and absentmindedly doodled in the margins. It wasn't that I had writer's block — I knew exactly what I wanted to write. I even knew the words I wanted to use. I was just too distracted to write.

I fiddled with the story for a while, drawing a diagram on one of the pages. Thoughts raced through my head as I examined the possibilities. *If I put the character in this situation, would it fulfill the character arc? What could I do to make the rising action peak to the climax more successfully? Will the character growth satisfy the story?*

I had to look at the story in a professional way. I couldn't let this become personal. I tried to analyze the story and Faith as if they were no more than letters on a page — flat, two-dimensional, and predictable. If I looked at the story that way, then maybe I wouldn't have to make sense of the personal connection I felt with Faith.

But there was no changing this. Faith was real, and Salem was real, too. So were all the other people in it. My characters were no longer characters — they were people, with real feelings and real faces.

I would never look at my story the same way again. It had changed me. I didn't want anything bad to happen to Faith, but if nothing did, what would that do to my story? What would happen to Faith and her family if I simply stopped writing, if I never finished it? Would they just disappear, cease to exist? Or would they freeze as they were written, unable to experience anything other than what the last words I had written dictated?

I had learned something. Stories were nothing like I had thought them to be. Words weren't either. They were deeper, more complex — full of emotions, complexities and life.

Unpredictable

Sensations

Intricate

I wrote more of the story, writing as if nothing had changed. Because I couldn't let it change. One word after another, a string of letters on paper. Simple. Easy. Nothing more.

The pages filled slowly and steadily. I let the words come, and I didn't stop to filter out the ones that weren't quite perfect. I knew they were already right as they were. And there was something about writing in ink: it couldn't be erased. Even though the words could be crossed out or covered, they could never truly be gone.

The story unfolded into the rising action, the point that led to the climax. Once I had written the climax, there would be no undoing it. I wasn't sure whether I even wanted to write it. Would my words set Faith Gray's life in stone? I couldn't be sure, but for now I just avoided the thought and continued writing as planned.

It was the only thing I knew how to do.

Chapter Ten

As each day went by, people progressively began to talk to me less and less. I zoned out at the kitchen table, and although Hazel and I saw each other in school every day, I never stopped to talk with her for more than a few minutes. Everyone noticed the change in me, but they likely attributed it to my recent disappearance, which I tried to avoid talking about when I could. I knew the real reason that I inadvertently withdrew from conversations and found myself no longer taking walks in the park.

My story was beginning to consume my life.

I hadn't flashed into my story again, even though I had tried to will myself into it. It seemed to only happen when my story wanted it to, if such a thing was possible, and I didn't have any control over it. It meant that any time of the day, no matter what I was doing, I could flash out of existence in this world, whether I was in the middle of a crowd, in school giving a presentation, or on the highest floor of a skyscraper. I may have been the writer, but I was not in control.

So it was fortunate that I happened to be in my room at my desk once again when I felt that familiar sensation. I was just finishing writing the rising action of my story and was about to start the climax when my head began to throb.

It was much faster this time. I dropped my pen midsentence and started to close my journal out of habit. I barely had enough time to grab Faith's dress draped over the back of my chair with my other hand before the world blurred and the sound of the ticking of the wall clock in my room ceased.

Ephemeral

This time, I found myself sprawled across a wooden floor. I banged my head against the hard boards and barely bit back a yelp of pain. A mere foot away from my shoulder was a thick, woven rug. Why couldn't I have landed on that instead?

The sound of footsteps echoed on the floor, and I shot to my feet. I was in a bedroom, but it was not one I had seen before. There was a single bed with a blue quilted cover spread over it and a sturdy chest that sat at the foot of the bed. In the corner of the room stood a small table that held a washbasin and a pitcher. The pitcher was ornately decorated and stood out in the otherwise drab room, but it was obviously not modern.

Relic

Other than those few pieces of furniture, though, the room was bare.

Fortunately, the room was also vacant—no one had witnessed my appearance.

I glanced around the room for a second time, noticing several items that I had overlooked the first time. Faith's dress had been tossed across the room and lay crumpled in the corner by the washbasin, but at least I had been able to hang on to it long enough for it to travel here with me. But the item at my feet made me gasp as I bent down to retrieve it.

It was my writing journal. I picked it up and smoothed the pages, unfolding one corner that had become dog-eared. How had it gotten here?

I thought back to the moments before I had flashed here. I had started to close the book, but had I finished before I had been hurled into the past? I couldn't be sure, but I must have still been holding on to it, because here it was.

After another quick glance to confirm that no one was around, I slid Faith's dress over my head to cover the jeans and Disneyworld t-shirt I was wearing. I could only imagine people's reactions to such an ensemble.

Once I managed to secure the ties at the back of my dress, I slid my journal into one of the dress pockets and checked to make sure it was completely concealed. It was fortunate that the pockets were large—the journal created only the slightest bulge in the fabric.

Concealment

Now I knew that whatever I was holding could travel here with me. I hadn't even considered the possibility before. What else was there for me to learn about falling through time?

Voices came from outside the room and footsteps made the floor vibrate as someone moved through the house. The footsteps began to grow louder. If I wasn't careful, I was going to be discovered. I dashed from the bedroom, out into the hallway, and into the room next to it, not stopping to check if it was occupied. After stopping to quiet the frantic beating of my heart, I looked around. A wide-eyed boy stared back at me.

It most certainly was occupied.

"It's okay!" I said to the boy quickly. "I—uh—I mean you no harm."

The boy struggled to a standing position. "How did you manage to get inside without being seen?" The boy looked at me with bright blue eyes full not of suspicion, but of curiosity.

I realized then that I had seen this boy before. It was William, Faith's brother. I looked around the room carefully and discovered it was the bedroom Faith and her brother shared. The curtain had been pulled back, but I wasn't as familiar with William's side. "I didn't sneak in," I tried to tell William. "I was invited."

William only laughed. "Father is at a neighbor's farm, grinding grain. He is a miller. And Mother and Faith have not left the hearth in hours." He didn't need to point out the obvious — that no one could have invited me in.

I started to stutter out some kind of excuse, but William cut in. "I know you. You are the girl who ate supper with us. Faith's friend." I nodded and William continued. "You eat rather strangely."

I had to laugh at that.

"Should I fetch Faith for you?" William suggested.

I blinked. This was certainly easier than finding myself in Salem Town, miles away from Salem Village, and having to walk the entire distance to find Faith. "Sure — I mean, please do," I corrected myself hastily.

William dashed off to the kitchen, where I heard him speaking excitedly. How much did he know about me? Certainly Faith wouldn't share with him the fact that I could disappear into thin air.

William returned with Faith in tow. "Here she is!" he exclaimed in obvious excitement. "Do not fear, I only said that I had found Faith's missing Sabbath dress. She knew what I meant right away, and Mother nearly fainted in relief!" William seemed to relish the fact that he was involved in a secret meeting.

Surreptitious

Faith gave me a wide smile. "I had to take the wooden stirring spoon from her hands, lest she drop it into the boiling pot of stew for supper!"

"Oh, I'm so sorry, Faith. I didn't mean to take your dress with me, truly."

Faith waved a hand in the air in dismissal. "Oh, no matter. It gave me an excuse to wear my everyday dress to church, anyhow. My good dress is so scratchy I can hardly bear it! I do not know how you can."

Laughing, I had to admit that it was a bit uncomfortable.

Cumbersome

Mrs. Gray called out something from the kitchen, and William scampered away. In silent agreement, Faith and I moved into the hallway, heading outside where we could speak more freely. As we headed to the hill behind the house, I examined the village. Not much had changed since I had last seen it. It was quiet, and it seemed as though fewer people lingered on the streets than before. The patches of snow on the ground had disappeared, though, and the air was dusty and dry.

The sun beat down on my back, making me wish I didn't have to wear Faith's dress, which was made of such heavy material that it seemed like it was meant for wintertime.

I watched as Faith rubbed her hands up and down her arms in rapid motions. "What's the matter?"

"Oh." Faith looked away. "I do not know, really. Ofttimes, I feel little prickles run along my limbs. Almost like when I prick myself with a needle, only these are repeated. It is strange. The other girls say they feel it too, all the time, except it gets worse—I do not know. I cannot help but think…"

Faith trailed off, but I knew what she was going to say. She thought it was the witches, slowly tormenting her. It was a symptom that even the unaffected people experienced throughout the course of the Witch Trials. It was an inexplicable phenomenon.

Faith and I settled ourselves on the grass on the side of the hill that faced away from the houses, away from the prying eyes of Mrs. Gray and the others. I looked at Faith in expectance. "So, what have I missed?"

Faith became unexpectedly somber. "There has been much excitement." She looked anything but excited though. "Whilst you were gone, the most awful things occurred. You recall our neighbor, Bridget Sutton, do you not?"

I nodded. The woman who had brought me and Faith to the meetinghouse, then later shouted at us in the night and chased us down the road.

"She is dead."

"What?"

"She was hanged a while ago. She was tried for witchcraft and found guilty, so she was hanged. And five more people have been convicted," Faith added.

Faith's face was blank and her words were merely factual, and though I watched her guarded expression carefully, I couldn't tell what she was feeling. When Faith spoke again, though, the quiver in her voice betrayed her emotions. "Her own daughter accused her. Mary Sutton—I know her well. How could she kill her own mother?"

She choked back a sob, and I looked away, stunned. How could the girl I had spoken to at the Parris house be capable of doing such a thing? These girls used to be such nice people, but playing with fire had changed them. The power they had gained over their town had corrupted them.

"Faith, what is today's date?"

She blinked away a few stray tears, looking slightly startled. "It is the nineteenth of July."

I was afraid of that. I took a sharp intake of breath, but Faith didn't seem to notice.

Faith began to speak again, but her tone had changed as she forced herself to put on a more cheerful countenance. "Shall we go into town now? It is a good time for it. Mother is in the kitchen preparing our meal, and she no longer needs my assistance."

"No!" I said the word more forcefully than I had intended, and Faith flinched. "You do *not* want to witness the five hangings today, trust me on this."

"What? How did you know there were to be five hangings today?"

Oops. I had discovered that during my research—the first of the accused was hanged in June. Then there were five hangings in July, all on the same day: July 19, 1692.

I was tired of telling lies. For the past week, Faith had been the friend to me that no one else could be—not even Hazel anymore, who was very different than me. I realized then that I wanted to tell Faith the truth—the whole truth.

"Faith, remember how I keep disappearing right in front of your eyes at strange times?"

Faith nodded immediately, brow furrowed. She'd probably wanted to ask me about that for a while. That was one of the things I liked about her—she didn't pry.

"Well, that's my way of traveling…home. I don't do it on purpose, but it just happens."

Faith shook her head. "I am afraid I do not understand."

I was not explaining this very well. I tried again. "Where I come from, the events of today have already happened. I looked them up and found information on this day, the nineteenth of July in the year sixteen hundred and ninety-two." Suddenly, I remembered my writing journal, which I pulled out from my pocket. I turned to the first page, where I had drawn a timeline of the events that happened in real life in Salem. I had drawn one next to it that represented each major event in my story, so I could compare how accurate my story was historically. I showed it to Faith and pointed at the day, *July 19.*

Faith stared at it for a moment uncomprehendingly. "Oh." She shook her head, her confusion evident. "Where did you come by this book?" She suddenly became vehement. "Mercy, that is not the Devil's book, surely?"

I laughed. Of course any person here would come to that conclusion. "No, it's not. Isn't the Devil's book supposed to be red?"

"Oh, that is true." Faith began to skim through the story timeline. I followed her eyes as they scanned the page, until she gasped. She pointed a trembling figure at the page. "Why is my name here?" She started to look at the next page, where the timeline continued past the day of July 19. I hastily snapped the book closed. I couldn't let her see what my story's future held for her.

"Why is my name on this list of yours?" Faith

repeated. She was calm, but something else flickered across her face. I couldn't tell if it was fear, confusion, or anger.

I took a deep breath. It was time to tell her.

Reveal

I had kept the secret long enough. "Faith, I like to write things. Stories. For enjoyment."

Comprehension dawned on Faith's face and she looked a bit relieved. "Is that all? You write, like in school, but for pleasure?"

"Yes. But there's more. One day I started writing a particular story. I just made it up, from my imagination. I simply started writing, and then somehow, I felt myself being pulled away, like you saw me when I disappeared on your doorstep the first time I met you, and again behind the Parris house."

Faith nodded for me to continue, watching me expectantly. I doubted she was going to like this. I spoke once more, then waited for her reaction.

"The story I've been writing is about a girl named Faith. She has dark brown hair and gray eyes, lives in Salem Village in the year sixteen hundred and ninety-two, and wants to travel, just like you. But it's more than that. She *is* you." I hurried on, desperate to explain. "I wrote about the town and the people and how everyone started to become fearful that their own neighbors were witches. Some of what I wrote actually happened. I researched this time and place in history and wrote my story around all of this, Faith. I don't know how, but as I created these words, in some twisted sort of fate, I became a part of it too. It's your story, but it's also mine. I'm the writer."

Faith's face was stony and expressionless, but when she opened her mouth to speak, it was as if a dam had broken. "What kind of fool do you take me for? Is this some kind of trick you have devised to poke fun at me? I thought you were my friend." She returned to her calm, stoic demeanor that scared me so much. "I am sorry, but I simply cannot believe you."

I had been guessing she might say that, but I had hoped otherwise. There was only one thing I could show her that could get her to believe what I said.

Proof

"Look." I spoke the word softly, but when I took out my journal, I turned the pages haphazardly until I found a scene that featured her. I had to make her understand.

"I wrote this scene a week ago. It has already happened for you, so I think you'll recognize it."

I handed her the journal and she took it as if it might burst into flames at any moment. As her eyes traveled across the page, I followed them, reciting in my mind the words I had committed to memory:

Faith had decided that morning to go to the witch examination, but now she wished she hadn't. The afflicted girls were soaking up the attention, and there was always someone in the crowd willing to catch them when their tormentors made them fall to the floor.

"Bridget Sutton, why do you harm these girls?"

"I do not. I am innocent."

The girls' bodies distorted into positions that were so terrible that Faith couldn't watch them. She looked away.

"These girls say you lie."

Bridget shook her head vehemently. "I am no witch. I am innocent."

"I do not believe she did those things." Faith said the words quietly, to no one in particular.

The woman beside her blanched. "Whatever do you mean, child? Of course she did."

After she had read the last word, Faith looked up at me. I could tell by how pale her face had become that this was one of the events she had experienced. "You were not here when this event occurred. You could not have known," Faith said softly, as if she was speaking to herself. She raised her eyes to look at me. "Who are you?" A strange expression crossed her face.

It pained me to see her look at me like that, like I was a stranger.

Throb

"I'm Tess, just as I told you. You know me—I haven't changed."

Faith didn't seem to hear me. "So, all of this was a lie. I trusted you. When the other girls spoke of you behind your back, I defended you. I *protected* you." She cut herself off abruptly and started again. "You are telling me that I owe my existence to *you*? All of this—my entire life—is nothing more than a story? You say that I am not real—just a character that you may do with as you please?"

She shook my journal in my face. "This book tells me that none of this is real, that everything I thought I knew is false. The ink is on the page, plain as day, yet I still cannot quite believe it. Mercy, I do not wish to believe it." She let out a strangled cry that sounded like a sob, though her eyes were dry.

"Faith." I rested a hand on her shoulder, but she jerked away as if she had been burned.

"Faith," I pleaded again. "Please. Just because I found you in my imagination doesn't mean that you're not real. I don't understand how it works, but I imagined you just as you are, and when I was pulled into my story and into your life in this century, here you were. Just because I wrote about you doesn't mean you don't exist."

"No! You cannot determine my life. I am the person I want to be, not the person you wrote me to be." She stood up, pressing her lips tightly together. "I no longer know you. I thought we were friends, but it appears that we never were."

Faith ran from me, clutching my journal in both hands.

Chapter Eleven

Scrambling to my feet, I followed Faith as she disappeared down the hill. "Faith, wait! Our friendship was real. It always has been!"

I caught sight of Faith dashing to the bridge that crossed a river on the other side of the hill. Her hair loosened from the knot at the nape of her neck and streamed behind her as she ran. The pages of my journal flapped in the wind as Faith raced to the river, still grasping the book. She stopped at the very edge of the riverbank, briefly looking back at me only once.

Brink

I knew immediately what she was going to do.

"No! Please, Faith, no!"

Faith whipped her head away and raised one

hand, still holding the book, over her head. Just as I reached her, gasping for breath, she threw my journal deep into the raging water of the river. "What have you done?" I gasped, eyes wide.

When Faith looked at me, her eyes were blank and dead. "Something no less than that devilish book deserves." She turned and fled, and in my shock I let her go.

I unfroze once she disappeared across the bridge, heading in the direction of Salem Town. She was probably going to meet with her new friends, Ann Putnam and Deliverance Johnson.

Bitter

But I had no time to waste thinking about Faith. Dashing to the edge of the water, I found a forked stick and used it to probe the water's surface. The journal had sunk to the bottom. Faith had thrown the journal several feet in, so there was no way I could reach it without getting wet.

I plunged into the frigid water, not bothering to lift my skirts that had become heavy with water and silt. I was in water up to my thighs, but I plunged my hands into the depths, desperately searching for my journal. *Come on, come on,* I pleaded silently. The freezing water was numbing, but I hardly noticed in my frantic search for the book.

My fingers brushed against something hard and

angular. Holding my breath, I fished the object out of the water. It was my journal.

Only when I held my journal in my hands did I let out the breath I had been holding. I trudged out of the river and onto the bank, lifting my feet high. I hurried to dry ground and sank to my knees in the long grass, carefully opening the book, afraid of what I would find. Could it be salvaged?

Some of the pages had turned to pulp and most were stuck together in thick clumps. The leather cover was mostly intact, but I was more worried about the pages inside than the actual book itself. A book could be replaced, but the words inside could not. On the few pages I could turn, most of the words were still readable, but I'd have to dry each page individually to have any hope of saving it.

The first few pages could not be saved, though. These were the pages where I had done the planning and outlining for my story, and I could no longer see the charts or words. Strangely, the two pages with the timelines I had shown Faith just moments ago were completely blank. They were soggy, like the rest of the pages, but as far as I could tell the words on them had completely disappeared.

Void

Even stranger, the very last page in the book, the one that I had filled with meaningful words for many years, was completely unharmed. The writing was still legible and the paper wasn't as wet as most of the other pages. I felt a strange sense of relief that at least that page had been spared. I knew most of my words I had collected by heart, but it was a comfort to still have them preserved on paper.

The rest of the pages were stuck together in one stiff mass. I couldn't tell just yet if my story had been harmed, or if there was anything left of it to read at all. What would that do to the real story, the one that was playing out in front of me?

Something about these pages that held the written words of my story had given life to the story and triggered my travels to Salem. I didn't think I could recreate that. It was the power of these words that had brought me here, and now the words may have been destroyed. If I couldn't save these pages, what would happen to my connection with Faith? And just as important, if my words were gone, how would I ever get home?

These were not pleasant thoughts to dwell on. A noise suddenly came from behind me, and I jumped. Had Faith returned?

When I looked over my shoulder, I saw that it was an older gentleman who had stopped to watch me. He eyed me in confusion. "What are you doing, child? Are you praying?"

I was still kneeling in the grass, holding my journal in front of me. Maybe he thought it was a Bible. After merely staring back at him for a moment, I nodded. It was the easiest way to get him to leave.

The man nodded briskly, and understanding and relief dawned on his face. Evidently, that was the most believable explanation.

"Mayhap I can suggest that you go to the church, then?" the man advised helpfully.

"Oh. Oh yes, I'll be sure to do that. Thank you."

Finally the man left, taking off his hat briefly to wipe the perspiration from his forehead when he thought no one was watching.

I stood, brushing stray blades of grass from my dress. I couldn't just stay here. Any more lingering would cause suspicion. But where would I go? I doubted I would be welcome in the Grays' house anymore, even if Faith wasn't home at the moment.

I was almost positive she had gone to Salem Town, the exact place I had advised her not to go, just to show me that she could do as she liked. I wished that what I had revealed to her had gone over better, but there was no remedying that. The good thing about writing was that the author could always change the story and improve it, taking out scenes and rearranging chapters.

But this story didn't seem to work like that. Once something was written, it was there forever, etched onto the paper and the hearts of the characters. But even so, things didn't always come out the way I meant them to. In fact, I was discovering that they rarely did.

I began to walk purposefully now, tucking my damp journal into my pocket. I knew where I was going to go while I waited to flash back into my own world.

The roads in Salem Town were crowded with people when I arrived out of breath two hours later. I knew without asking why everyone was here — they wanted to witness the hangings of five women.

Spectacle

A woman next to me was gossiping about how horrible it was that Rebecca Nurse had been discovered to be a witch. "I never would have known if not for those poor children. Rebecca was always such a sweet lady. Did you know she is a grandmother? It only proves that the Devil is truly a trickster."

Her companion nodded in agreement. Normally, women would be severely punished for gossiping of any kind. They would each be forced to wear a brank, an instrument with an iron cage that fit over the head. Attached to it was a piece of metal that was shoved into the person's mouth. It pressed down hard on the tongue, making the wearer unable to speak.

But today must have been an exception. Everyone was too busy to notice the women gossiping. In fact, nearly everyone was whispering among themselves anyway. A big event such as this was sure to bring most of the townspeople to the scene.

I kept walking as the crowd thickened. This was the outskirts of town, where the buildings were few and scattered, yet the area was crammed with townspeople. I pushed through the crowds, searching for a single face. I wasn't thrilled to be so close to the place where five human beings' necks were about to be snapped, but I had no choice. This was where everyone else was.

Just then I caught a flash of a familiar gray dress. There was nothing significant about it — dozens of people nearby wore nearly identical ones — but I knew in an instant that it was Faith.

Pushing through the crowds, I tailed her, staying just far enough behind that she wouldn't fall out of sight. Though she may have given up on me, I certainly hadn't given up on her. I had to make sure she was going to be okay.

Loyalty

As I rounded a corner, I realized I shouldn't have worried. Faith stood with a group of girls in a circle, laughing. I glowered at the back of one girl's head.

One of the girls in the group was Deliverance.

I happened to be watching her when one of her hands twitched, and then her whole body began to convulse. She let out a bloodcurdling scream. The girl next to her began spouting something nonsensical. She jabbered on, saying words that I could not understand.

One by one, all the girls in the group screamed out in pain or fell to the ground. But now I was only watching Faith.

She rubbed her hands up and down her arms in quick motions, just as I had seen her do earlier. Then she flinched and whirled around, but no one was behind her. From where I stood, I could plainly see the pain in her eyes and I watched her as she bit down on her lip, hard. She showed more restraint than the rest of the girls, but her pain looked genuine.

The girls' afflictions caused some attention from the people in the crowd nearest to them. "Do not fear!" one of the people in the crowd called out to the girls. "In but a few moments, the ones who do you harm will do so no more."

The crowd shifted, and suddenly I had a clear view of a large tree, which stood at the top of a hill. It was Gallows Hill, I realized with horror. This was the hanging tree.

As I watched, five blindfolded people, hands tied behind their backs, were taken from a cart and led to a platform beneath the tree where five waiting ropes hung slack from the largest branch.

Four of the accused witches were stoic and stiff as they climbed the steps and waited silently.

Torpor

My eyes were fixed on the other woman. Although her eyes were hidden, I could see her mouth, which, even from this distance, I noticed trembled slightly.

I couldn't watch anymore. I spared one glance to make sure Faith was all right—she stood a little away from the other girls now, a horrified expression on her face as she stared, transfixed, at the accused witches by the hanging tree. Then I hurried away, not stopping when I accidentally trod on someone's foot and his protests rang after me.

I tripped on the hem of my dress but quickly righted myself. I felt guilty about leaving Faith alone in the square, but I mentally assured myself she would be okay. She was a strong girl. She could handle calamities, and she had certainly had her share of them so far.

The colors around me blurred together into one bright mass as I finally broke through the crowd. The world spun as I was thrown off of my feet and flung from my story and back to my own time.

In every other instance, I had found myself back in my room, but this time a world in white greeted me when I opened my eyes. Biting cold chilled my skin, and I lay on something wet and slushy.

Jumping up, I dusted the snow from my body. It was quite the change, going from broiling heat to snow in a matter of moments.

Thankfully, I recognized my surroundings. I was only in my backyard, not someplace foreign to me, as I had feared. Something had changed when I brought my journal with me instead of having it to come back to, but at least I was someplace familiar.

I *did* have my book, didn't I? I rifled through the pocket of Faith's dress for one frightening moment, but then I felt the distinctive texture of my leather journal. With relief, I withdrew my hand and wriggled out of the dress. I still wore my own clothes beneath it. Balling up the dress in my hands, I hurried up the steps to try the back door, which, as I had hoped, was unlocked.

As I passed the living room, Mom greeted me casually. Obviously I hadn't been gone long—that was a relief. Mom sat in a leather armchair, curled up beneath a blanket reading one of her teaching manuals. That was light reading for her.

"When did it start snowing?" I asked her, and Mom marked her place in her book with her finger so she could look up at me.

"Oh, probably an hour or so ago. The weatherman says it's going to snow for the rest of the day. We may get over a foot of snow."

I nodded in distraction, no longer thinking about the snow. I was anxious to get up to my room and examine my journal for further damage. Maybe more of the pages would be unstuck by now.

I spent the next hour in the upstairs bathroom my parents and I shared, drying each individual page with a hair dryer.

Restoration

It was tedious business, but effective. Once I had finished, the pages were dry and no longer stuck to each other, though they had become a bit stiff and wrinkled from the water damage.

Thankfully, most of the pages in my journal still contained ink that was readable, even the ones in the middle that had been stuck together in a big block of pulpy paper. The only ones that could not be saved, I confirmed, were the beginning pages, whose words I still could not see. Not even the faintest shadow of ink remained on those pages.

I sat at my desk once again, flipping to the pages I had not yet filled. Only twenty pages remained—just enough to finish my story.

This was it. This was the moment that I had to decide whether I finished the story as I had originally planned, or gave it all up. The climax. These words, even more than the others I had written so far, would condemn Faith to whatever future was determined for her.

I had made my decision. I had to finish this, no matter what the cost. My pen hovered over the page, and I could not stop my hand from shaking just the tiniest bit.

Just before the tip of my pen touched the page, I stopped.

Hesitation

"I'm sorry, Faith," I whispered softly.

And I began to write.

Chapter Twelve

When the ending was complete, I simply sat there for a moment, staring at the final words: "The End."

I didn't know what to feel. I couldn't make my fingers move to turn the pages to look back at what I had written. My journal was completely full now — I'd had to cram the words together to make them fit.

Complete

Suddenly, a strong sense of trepidation curdled inside me, making my head shoot up in surprise. The feeling was nothing like the dread and uncertainty I had felt as I penned the last words. This was something more.

The feeling wouldn't go away. It nagged and pulled at me, forcing me to give it attention. There was something very wrong. Somehow, I knew that Faith needed me. I didn't know how I knew — the only thing I knew for certain was that I had to act immediately, before time ran out.

I changed into Faith's dress quickly. Too quickly, I realized, when the fabric tore at the elbow. Not bothering to examine the tear, I grabbed my cell phone from the table beside my bed. Tapping my foot with impatience, I waited for it to turn on and load the starting screen. Once the screen lit up, I began to type a message to Hazel, fingers flying over the keys, then thought better of it and pressed the key to speed-dial her number instead.

Hazel answered on the second ring. "Tess! You finally called me. So, did you decide to take me up on my—"

"Sorry, Hazel," I cut her off, knowing I would feel guilty later. "It's kind of an emergency. Do you think— could you cover for me? If my mom calls, can you tell her that I'm over there with you? That we're having a sleepover or something? It's important."

There was silence for a moment. I was jittery, nearly jumping up and down in my impatience. The static on the other end crackled as Hazel breathed into the phone. Finally Hazel sighed. "You're not going to tell me what's going on, are you?"

I started to tell her that I'd explain everything to her soon, but she broke in. "I'll do it."

I grinned and lifted the phone away from my ear as I started to hang up. Hazel spoke again. "Girl, you owe me big, though!"

After she had hung up, I jabbed the end call button and stuffed the cell phone into my pocket. The insistent, urgent feeling hadn't gone away. I had to hurry. Squeezing my eyes shut tight, I tried to imagine myself being tossed into my story, as I had been so many times before. For the first time ever, I wished for a headache. "Come on, come on," I mumbled as I tried unsuccessfully to flash into the past. Nothing worked. Naturally, the one time that I actually wanted to hurl myself into my story, I couldn't.

My temper flared and I lost control of it. "I am the author!" I shrieked at the air. "Let me in!" I paused for a moment, but no feelings of dizziness came. Dejected, I collapsed in my desk chair, resting my fingers on the still-open journal in front of me.

Suddenly, electricity sizzled through my veins, a sensation unlike anything I had ever experienced. Pain shot through my body. It had never hurt this much before. It was as if my body collided with a barrier, though I felt no movement. A deep, deafening noise filled my ears, then subsided and vanished as quickly as it had come.

When I opened my eyes, my room had been

replaced by a landscape dotted with clusters of buildings. Still off balance, I stumbled backward, crashing into a brick wall. Somehow I managed to stay on my feet, and I collected myself quickly.

I was in Salem Town. The building I had bumped into was the courthouse. Good — I had a feeling that was exactly where I needed to be.

Instead of walking, I ran. Immediately, it became evident that although I was wearing Faith's dress, I had once again forgotten to put on shoes, so I felt each individual pebble in the road dig into the soles of my feet through my socks. There wasn't anything I could do about it now, though.

I reached the top of the steps that led up to the courthouse and burst through the doors, ignoring the masses of people who protested when I pushed them aside in my haste. I found my way to a gap in the crowd and stopped there. Immediately, my eyes found Faith, who stood near the center of the room, looking small. The crowd chattered to themselves quietly, but all eyes were trained on her.

Solitary

A man wearing a long, white wig sat behind a tall stand, looking imperiously down at Faith. A nameplate on the stand read: *Chief Justice William Stoughton.* "Faith Gray. Tell us why you have hurt these girls."

Faith was frozen in fear. "I have told you, I-I did no such thing." She tugged on her everyday gray dress to smooth out the wrinkles.

Cries arose from one side of the room, where, I noticed for the first time, Ann Putnam and the rest of her group stood. They began tugging at their dresses and their bodies contorted horribly. When Faith turned her head to stare at them, their heads turned sharply to the side in unison.

I spotted the rest of the Gray family in the crowd, standing in a corner far from Faith. Mr. and Mrs. Gray were holding William back, and I could see the fear in Mrs. Gray's eyes. But it wasn't fear *for* Faith, I realized. It was fear *of* her.

"Why do you lie?" Stoughton narrowed his eyes at her. The record keeper at his side scribbled furiously on a sheet of paper.

Faith shook her head. Ann and the girls did the same. "I do not lie. I speak the truth!" When she blinked, the girls fell to the floor as if they were no more than puppets on a string.

"Her spirit pinches and taunts us!" Deliverance cried, pointing an accusing finger at Faith. Gasps arose from the crowd, but Faith was smart enough to stay quiet.

The judge started to ask Faith something, but I was no longer listening. "She's suspected of witchcraft."

I hardly realized that I'd spoken the words aloud. "What have I done?" I whispered.

When I wrote the end of my story, it didn't seem real. It was just ink on paper. Now I understood what I had done, though. It was one thing to write about this event on paper. It was another to witness the consequences of my words right before my eyes.

A man standing beside me seemed to overhear part of what I said, and he turned to me. "It is more than mere suspicion that she aroused," the man said. "It is a certainty, now. Have you not heard what the witch did that exposed her involvement with the Devil? Why, she accused those poor girls themselves of evil-doing! For a time I believed she was afflicted too, but it is now clear that was only trickery on her part. She actually accused those girls, saying they were the ones who caused trouble. Well, I can tell you she will most certainly be found guilty. As soon as her doings were discovered, she was jailed to await this trial."

A shiver ran through my whole body. This was all my fault. At that moment, Faith clenched her hands into fists and spoke, not seeming to notice the girls, who cried out that she was digging her nails into their skin and they could see the marks.

"Let me tell you that I am completely innocent of this crime of which they have accused me!" Faith's voice shook with anger, but it was strong, echoing throughout the room that had gone silent. "These girls accuse their very neighbors, and now they even accuse the prominent people of this town. Do you not find that suspicious?"

Silence stifled the room and the people it held. For the most part they looked unconvinced. Many of the people were staring daggers at Faith. But there were a few that looked doubtful, considering what Faith had said.

Hope

Chief Justice Stoughton tried to call a witness to the stand to testify, but Faith continued speaking, raising her voice as if daring someone to stop her.

"Mayhap some of the girls were ill at first, but it is plain to me now that they are not afflicted. The named witches that were hanged on June tenth, July nineteenth and the days since then are all innocent. These girls are the ones who should be punished. These girls have fooled the lot of you. Their fits are merely tricks — they are the ones who lie. I was one of them before, but I can be no more. Believe not what they say, for I speak the truth — I swear to it!"

Ann suddenly screamed a blood-chilling scream and fell to the floor, eyes rolling back into her head. The other girls began to twitch and stumbled as they tried to stay on their feet.

Angry voices filled the room, and I barely noticed

when the judge declared that no more witnesses were necessary, and then the jury was out.

In an instant I was at Faith's side. "What are you doing? You should not be here." Faith hissed at me in a frantic whisper, eyeing the people around us, though they took no notice of me. "They have lost their senses!"

"That's why I'm here."

"For that I am glad." Faith was suddenly struggling to hold back tears. "Tess, do you know what they did to Felicity?"

Her cat. I put my hand on Faith's shoulder, trying to calm her, but she was almost hysterical.

"They slaughtered her! They said her offense was that she aided the Devil, but she did no such thing. She was only a cat!" The tears Faith had been holding back came forth now. "And now they think I am a witch too."

Before I could say anything, several men grabbed Faith and pulled her away, toward the doors. "Faith!" I called out to her, but the crowd jostled me and I could no longer see her.

"They will bring her back when the jury returns," someone near me said, but I was not comforted.

Much too soon, the jury returned and the room quieted. Faith had been brought back into the courthouse, and she stood alone in the middle of the room, fidgeting. Her eyes met mine, and I gave her what was meant to be an encouraging smile.

The judge addressed the jury. "What say you? What verdict have you reached?"

"Guilty."

No! My heart hammered in my chest, and I was frozen in place.

The judge rose in his seat. "Gentlemen, I think we are all in agreement as to the fate of this named witch. She has not confessed her guilt, and therefore cannot be pardoned. Faith Gray, I hereby sentence thee to death by hanging."

The crowd roared, but I barely heard them over the pounding of blood in my ears. Before I knew what I was doing, I rushed forward to where Faith still stood alone. When she saw me, her eyes widened and she shook her head at me almost imperceptibly, but I ignored her. I would not let her be alone at a time like this. Especially since this event had been really all my doing. I had never imagined it would really happen like this.

I raised my voice loud enough to be heard throughout the whole room. "Faith Gray is innocent!"

A collective gasp came from the crowd. "Who art thou, stranger?" the judge demanded.

I glanced over at Ann and saw the recognition and shock in her eyes. "I am just that. A stranger. My name is of no importance. But Faith is innocent." I started to say I could prove it, too, but I cut myself off when

I realized there was no way I could. There wasn't anything I could say that would convince them that Ann and the other afflicted girls were responsible. I didn't even know for sure that they knew exactly what they were doing the whole time, but they had to be pretending right now.

Deception

Everyone stared at me in shock. Then Ann broke the silence. "There is a yellow bird on her shoulder!" She pointed one long, stiff finger straight at me. "It is the Devil's messenger. This stranger has come to bring ruin upon this town and instill witchcraft in the veins of our neighbors. She has turned our neighbors, who we named witches, into her own puppets for the Devil to use as he pleases. She is the witch who made us turn on each other because we knew not that the witches who tormented us were merely her puppets. She is the one who hurts us through the witches she commands!"

I stared at Ann, horrified. Surely no one would believe that. But the other girls shouted out in agreement, telling the crowd of the horrible things my specter was doing.

"Tess has done no such thing. They lie!" But Faith's words were swallowed by the angry protests of the crowd around us.

"Seize her!" boomed the judge, and two burly

men stepped from the crowd and each grabbed one of my arms, clenching me in their tight grasp. "We must check her for a witchmark."

I struggled and flailed, lashing out at the men who held me, but I was no match for them. They shoved me to one side and held me still. "Do not struggle, child," one of them muttered to me. His eyes seemed to hold a little kindness in them. "It will only make things worse for you."

Knowing I could do nothing to stop what ensued, I stilled. While the men held me, a woman was called forward to examine me. As she inspected my neck for the slightest blemish, I flushed crimson in humiliation. She moved on to my arms, pushing my sleeves up past my elbows.

She paused when she noticed the unusual shape of my birthmark on my left forearm. She had been working silently, but upon seeing the mark she shot me a look of utter disgust. "Here it is. The witchmark." She jabbed her finger at my arm and the crowd erupted in chatter, leaning forward to better see the mark.

"It is only a birthmark!" I cried, but my voice was lost in the chaos.

"One moment!" The second man holding me raised his hand in the air, and the crowd quieted. He reached into my dress pocket and pulled out an object in his closed hand. I had been so busy watching the woman inspecting me that I hadn't noticed one of the men eyeing the slight bulge in my pocket.

Slowly, he opened his fist to reveal my cell phone, which I had forgotten I still had with me. "What in heaven's name is this?"

Chapter Thirteen

Staring at my cell phone in astonishment, Chief Justice Stoughton came down from behind the stand and started toward me. Faith, still standing nearby, watched the men holding on to me with worry, while her eyes flickered toward my phone in confusion. Everyone came forward at once, all trying to take a closer look at it.

Pandemonium

"What is this most unusual object?" The judge turned my phone over in his hands after the man who had collected it from me had handed it to him. He fingered it for a moment and slid it open to reveal the keypad. He flinched, and then began tentatively pressing a few of the buttons. Suddenly, a tinny voice came through the speaker, just loud enough for me and those closest to Stoughton to hear. "Tess? Where are—"

I tried to suppress a smile, which was entirely inappropriate given the circumstances, but I couldn't help myself. He must have pressed the key I had set to speed-dial Hazel. Who knew I could call her from seventeenth-century Salem?

Stoughton cried out in surprise and dropped the phone, disconnecting the call when the phone hit the floor with a clatter that resounded throughout the entire room. "I heard the voice of a girl inside that object!" he cried out in disbelief.

A moment later, fast-paced music began to blare from my cell phone speaker. Hazel must have been calling me back, wondering what was going on. Several people flinched, and the crowd shrank away from the phone.

"That is most certainly an instrument of the Devil, or I know not what is." Stoughton turned toward the crowd. "What say you?"

"Make her pay for what she has done to our town!" one voice called out from among the rest. Everyone started to speak at once, yelling insults in my face. From somewhere in the crowd a shoe was thrown, and I ducked just before it hit me square in the face. Instead, it glanced off the side of my head, raising a nasty bump.

Angry voices filled my ears, but one voice rose above all the rest. "She must be condemned to immediate death for the sins she has committed."

The words struck me hard and I stared into the crowd dazed, but then the people around me began to shout in agreement and the men tugged me forward, pulling me outside. The crowd behind us pushed me forward, faster and faster. I stumbled on the hem of my dress and the men began to drag me while I tried to get to my feet.

Bleak

The shocked voice of Chief Justice Stoughton came from behind me. "Wait! We must handle this rationally. What about the trial and the death warrant that the law requires? There is no reason to be hasty!"

But he was swallowed by the crowd pouring out the doors and pushing me forward, and now I could no longer hear his voice.

I was able to take one glance over my shoulder. My phone had been left on the ground where it lay, discarded. It was the least of my worries now. I caught one glimpse of Faith, staring back at me in terror, pushing her way through the crowd to get to me, before I was thrust out into the open air.

During the time I'd been inside the courthouse it had begun raining, and now that there was no roof over me, I was drenched. Faith's dress stuck to my skin, and mud squelched beneath my feet, seeping through my socks. My feet quickly became ice-cold.

Frozen

I was rushed forward, but with all the people surrounding me I couldn't see where I was being taken. In my panic, I couldn't collect my thoughts and I tried desperately to figure out what to do.

We stopped abruptly and I tripped. Tasting mud in my mouth, I got to my feet, only to have my hands roughly tied behind my back. Suddenly there was a ladder in front of me, and someone prodded me from behind, forcing me to climb it.

Standing on the top rung of the ladder, I realized with horror where I was. I had seen this before, when I had witnessed the hangings on July nineteenth. But now I was looking at it from a different point of view.

I was about to be hanged.

The crowd rushed around the ladder upon which I stood and surrounded it as closely as they dared to go. They were anxious to see the show that was about to begin.

They didn't bother blindfolding me, so I had a clear view of all that was happening, which only served to frighten me more. At least if I'd been blindfolded, I wouldn't have to watch the sneering, gloating faces staring up at me.

Two men still held me tightly so that there was no

hope for escape. I stepped on one man's hand as hard as I could when he rested it on the ladder. Although he yelled and slapped me across the face with one hand, his grip didn't loosen enough for me to break away.

Someone reached up and slipped a rope around my neck. A noose. There was a noose around my neck and in moments I would be dead. A hysterical laugh burst from my throat.

Incredulity

I took a deep breath as the other end of the rope was being prepared. In the crowd, Faith pushed forward, only to stop helplessly when she reached the front. She looked at me, her face wracked with despair and grief, but she could do nothing. She and I both knew that. She looked at me for a long moment, and I met her eyes. Her gaze said all that she could not.

How ironic for my story to end this way, so twisted and so wrong. This wasn't how it was supposed to be. But at least Faith would be safe. She would be pardoned, I was sure of that. I faced the sky, trying to be brave.

I could do it. I could die for her.

All my life, I'd wanted to do something that mattered. I smiled at strangers in the street and gave children pushes on swings when no one else was around to do so. I gave away words to people who needed them.

None of it mattered now.

I had wished to write a story that was so real that it would mean something to the reader who read it. Now I finally had written a story that had been brought to life, and I had experienced it. I had somehow journeyed to a place where my story joined with the past, and I had become a part of it. I thought at first that I had done something impossible, something great. And now it was all falling apart.

I had collected ninety-nine words ever since I was old enough to understand them. *Desolation* threatened me when things got hard, but *bliss* took over. A *friend* changed me, and I learned to *believe*. *Wonder* kept me exploring, and *what if* challenged me to think. *Unpredictable* taught me that things can change, and *intricate* made me remember that we were all tied in an elaborate web of life.

And of course, *words* made all the difference.

I whispered my words to myself, lingering over each one.

Bright

Inspire

Truth

My words helped me understand my life. They helped me get through. As long as I had my words, I could handle anything.

Downpour

Enigma

Creations

Most of the people of Salem did not understand that their girls had found a great influence over them and used it. The day the first witch was accused, the girls began to understand the power of their own words. The accusations continued until they went so far that the words the girls spoke no longer mattered, because everyone had come to believe them. And here we were now.

Reminisce

Sensations

Forever

There was one last word that I had to add to my list:

Murder

The last thing I saw before I closed my eyes was Faith, looking at me intently through the rain spewing from the sky. The image lingered in my mind as the ladder I stood on was kicked out from under my feet. The rope, which was tied to a branch of the tree behind me, hung taut.

And the world exploded in pain.

Chapter Fourteen

Soft sheets brushed against my skin. Warmth seeped into my numb body, making my skin tingle. I became aware of my aching muscles, but I relished the discomfort because that meant I could feel something.

I moved my fingers slowly, testing each one to make sure they still worked. Someone at my side cried out, and voices spoke in hushed tones farther away.

It was a struggle to open my eyes. My eyelids felt heavy and swollen, and it took a great effort to open them just the tiniest bit. "Mom?" I croaked, blinking at the harsh light in the room. My voice startled me. It did not sound like my own—it was hoarse and rasping. My throat felt raw and unbelievably dry, as if it had been shredded and torn by the single word I had spoken.

A figure stood up and leaned over me. "Shh,

everything's all right." I blinked to clear my vision, which was blurred and distorted. A few strands of dark hair fell and hung over my face. It was Mom. I started to sit up, but I was too weak. My muscles failed and I collapsed against the pillow. Mom reached forward and helped me sit up carefully.

I was back in my own room, in my own bed. Mom had been sitting in a chair at my side, and Dad stood in the doorway with someone else by his side.

"Wh-what happened?" I choked the words out of my scratchy throat.

Mom tucked a limp strand of blond hair behind my ear. "Honey, we're not quite sure. Hazel told us you went to her house, but you must have been outside in the cold and snow for quite some time because you were soaked to the skin. Mr. Turner found you in our yard yesterday, collapsed in the snow." Mom gestured at the man standing by Dad, who I now recognized as our neighbor. Then Mom turned to look at me, brows pulled together in worry.

They had found me outside, in the snow? But that couldn't be true.

I pulled the covers back slightly. I was wearing my bright-colored pajamas. "Where's the dress?"

Mom looked confused. "What dress?"

I shook my head. "Never mind," I croaked.

She had a strange expression on her face. "And,

Tess," Mom hesitated, as if deciding whether she should tell me, "You were hurt when we found you. We think someone attacked you. Do you remember anything? You—you should see this." She held out a hand mirror, and I took it with shaking hands.

The eyes that stared back at me were sunken and shadowed, but I expected that. I tilted the mirror downward, and my breath caught. A deep, wide line cut across my neck. The skin was raised and raw, and it was puckered where angry gashes met the raised mark. I felt along my neck. The raised line continued all the way around, though it was worst in the front.

So it really had happened.

Words stuck in my throat, and I couldn't speak. Mom seemed to notice.

"We'll let you rest for a while, Tess. Let me know if you need anything; I'll be right down the hall. I'll check on you in a little while."

I could only nod. Mom and our neighbor left, but then Dad entered the room and settled on the edge of my bed. "Hey, honey." He gazed down at me fondly and I tried to smile back. "We were so worried." I looked down at my hands, which still clutched the mirror in my lap. I had worried them so much lately. When Dad saw the guilt in my eyes, he changed the subject. "I have something to show you."

He pulled a canvas from behind his back and

showed me. It was one of his paintings. A girl portrayed with soft colors stared back at me with gray eyes. I'd know that face anywhere. It was Faith. He had captured her perfectly, even though he had never met her. It was as though he somehow subconsciously knew to paint her eyes gray.

"It's your friend." Dad grinned hesitantly, as if he was unsure whether I would like it. "After you showed me your drawing of her—I don't know how else to explain it—I was inspired." He looked me in the eyes and spoke softly. "Maybe I won't throw this one away."

Dad left a few moments later, leaving the painting of Faith with me. As soon as the door closed softly behind him, I sat all the way up in my bed, gingerly feeling my throat.

When I managed to stumble out of bed, I grabbed a glass of water that someone had left on my desk, wincing when I gulped it down too fast and my throat throbbed.

Dad's painting of Faith still lay on my bedspread. I thought of Faith and all the others I had left behind.

My journal sat open in the middle of my desk. I settled myself into the seat, staring at the book. Somehow, my story had not let me die. The power of my words had saved my life, pushing me out of the past just in time. I was here, in my own world, but the raised scar on my neck was proof enough that the events in Salem had really happened.

The golden pen was missing from its place on my desk. It was no longer beside my journal. I searched the ground, but it seemed to have disappeared. What did that mean? Was the pen the catalyst that had made my story become reality? Or was it me? Maybe it didn't matter anymore. In some sort of twist of fate, words had come to me and merged together to create a story. No, it was more than a story.

My story and my experiences around it had changed me. Before I had thought that it was the words that made a story. Words were still infinitely important to me, but now I had discovered something even more important to a story — the people in it.

I used to spend all of my time writing alone. I hadn't realized that I had been neglecting the people around me — the people I loved. I'd thought that they didn't understand me, but in reality, I hadn't given them the chance to. I wouldn't make the same mistake again.

With my writing, I had done the impossible. I had made my story come to life, and it had shown me the value of a true friendship. A friendship that surpassed the boundaries of fiction and reality.

I remembered Mom's confusion at the mention of Faith's dress. I had not returned with it this time, which must mean the story was over. Somehow I knew that I would never return to Salem. I would never again see the characters I had come to know and love.

I hoped Faith and her family were safe now, wherever they were. The story had ended, but I couldn't bring myself to believe that their lives had ended too. I hoped with all my heart that they lived on, remaining with the historical figures in a past that I could never return to.

My eyes fell to the page that my book lay open to. The last page of the story.

I expected to see the familiar words I had written not so long ago, but somehow the words had changed. Even the words "The End" were no longer at the bottom of the page.

These words were not mine.

I blinked several times to make sure they were real. The words didn't disappear. A single paragraph filled the page, in handwriting different from mine. I read the words slowly, soaking them in:

> *As the sun cast shadows over the land,*
> *Faith watched from her position on the hill.*
> *Far off in the distance, a girl with blond hair*
> *and a denim jacket wove through the tall*
> *grass and disappeared around a bend. "No*
> *matter what," Faith whispered, "you and*

I will always have this friendship, which is stronger than the hatred that runs through this town. In friendship, we will never truly be far from each other's hearts."

I traced the words with my finger, reading them over and over again. This was Faith's way of saying goodbye. Somehow, with words, she had found a way. I pressed my fingertips to the page and let out a deep breath.

"I'll never forget you, either."

Tess's 100 Words

1. Desolation
2. Malone
3. Glitter
4. Skip
5. Grotesque
6. Pink
7. Bliss
8. Inspire
9. Friend
10. Maladroit
11. Success
12. Enigma
13. Lexicon
14. Conundrum
15. Words
16. Ink
17. Wanderlust
18. Muddled
19. Adrift
20. Zenith
21. Ethereal
22. Inundated
23. Vertigo
24. Illusions
25. Disarray
26. Reminisce
27. Forlorn
28-29. Déjà vu
30. Realization
31. Believe
32. Creations
33. Downpour
34. Questions
35. Bright
36. Insufficient
37. Wonder
38. Truth
39. Coincidence
40. Rhetoric
41. Slumber
42. Wonderstruck
43. Reality
44. Foreign
45. Shards
46. Respite
47. Barren
48. Recognition
49. Inquiries

50. Unison

51. Authority

52. Trepidation

53. Futile

54. Shackled

55. Ironic

56-57. What if

58. Forever

59. Serenity

60. Mischief

61. Possibilities

62. Burden

63. Silhouette

64. Repercussions

65. Astray

66. Plight

67. Saccharine

68. Premonition

69. Imminent

70. Flash

71. Lies

72. Mistakes

73. Unpredictable

74. Sensations

75. Intricate

76. Ephemeral

77. Relic

78. Concealment

79. Surreptitious

80. Cumbersome

81. Reveal

82. Proof

83. Throb

84. Brink

85. Bitter

86. Void

87. Spectacle

88. Loyalty

89. Torpor

90. Restoration

91. Hesitation

92. Complete

93. Solitary

94. Hope

95. Deception

96. Pandemonium

97. Bleak

98. Frozen

99. Incredulity

100. Murder

Author's Note

I have been fascinated by the Salem Witch Trials for a long time. I think what intrigues me the most about this time in history is the fact that no one knows what actually caused these events. While some believe that the girls were simply faking their afflictions, another theory is that the girls consumed ergot of rye, a bread fungus that is believed to cause hallucinations. Because of this mystery, I suppose it was only a matter of time before I decided to write a novel about it.

The reason I decided to have Tess write about the Salem Witch Trials is that I wanted her to experience a time period in which words were powerful. It was important to me to pick a setting that would complement Tess as a writer and her love for words. Whether or not the afflicted girls were truly afflicted, their words and actions were so convincing that most of the people in Salem believed them. In a time where girls were not given the freedom or attention that most adults received, having important members of the community listen to everything they said was invaluable.

Although *One Hundred Words* has many settings and characters based on history, it is a work of fiction. While I won't tell you what's fictional, I will talk about a few of the things that are real.

Salem Town and Salem Village were both real places. They were only a few miles apart, but several major rivers ran between them, making travel difficult. For the purpose of this book, I decreased the distance between the two and made it possible for Tess and Faith to more easily travel between them.

Many of the characters in *One Hundred Words* are based on the historical figures of the Salem Witch Trials. Chief Justice William Stoughton and Magistrate John Hathorne played a large part in the trials and examinations. Ann Putnam Jr., Abigail Williams, and Betty Parris were a few of the girls said to be afflicted.

Rebecca Nurse was one of the people accused of being a witch, and probably the most loved of the accused. Bridget Sutton, the Gray family's neighbor, is based on Bridget Bishop, a woman known for running a tavern and wearing a red bodice. In all, twenty people were executed in Salem, including one man who was pressed to death with stones.

My description of soap-making is true to the process that the Puritans used during that time. The brank, the metal instrument that circled the head and pressed on the tongue so the wearer couldn't speak, was an actual punishment. It was used to punish gossipers and was sometimes called the Gossip's bridle.

I used many, many resources during my research for this book, but one book that was vital for my research is *The Salem Witch Trials: A Day-by-Day Chronicle of a Community Under Siege* by Marilynne K. Roach. It documents the daily life and happenings in Salem and made it possible for me to coordinate certain days in my story with the actual days in 1692. For instance, in one case I was able to find out what the weather was like on a particular day.

If you are interested in learning more about the Salem Witch Trials, there are countless great books and online sites dedicated to this fascinating but tragic time in history. Here are just a few of the additional resources I used in the writing of this book:

Daily Life in Colonial America by Don Nardo

Salem Witch Trials Documentary Archive and Transcription Project: http://salem.lib.virginia.edu/home.html

The Devil on Trial: Witches, Anarchists, Atheists,

Communists, and Terrorists in America's Courtrooms by
Phillip Margulies and Maxine Rosaler

The Salem Witch Trials by Don Nardo

Witches: The Absolutely True Tale of Disaster in Salem
by Rosalyn Schanzer

Acknowledgments

I always thought the second book would be easier to write than the first one, but I've found that is certainly not the case! There aren't enough words for me to express how grateful I am to everyone who helped me turn this mere idea into a real book:

First of all, huge thanks goes to everyone at Parker Library. Thank you for giving people the wonderful gift of words. You guys inspire me to write stories that touch readers' hearts.

Heartfelt thanks to my editor Peggy Peterson, for the many hours spent helping me polish my words until they shone. Thank you for believing in my book.

Thanks to Shantana Judkins for working your magic once again to create this gorgeous cover. And to BookCrafters, my publishers, for not only putting all of the pieces together but also for cheering me on every step of the way.

To Rebecca, who helped me discover what true friendship is.

To all you authors, writers, and dreamers, who helped me believe that maybe I could do this too.

To everyone at NaNoWriMo and everyone who participated in the NaNoWriMo challenge along with me in years past. You convinced me that it is possible for a fifteen-year-old to write a novel in thirty days.

To my family, who compares my writing to that of bestselling authors whose works I could never hope to equal. Mom, thanks for sparking my interest in the Salem Witch Trials and putting up with my late-night "word sprints." Dad, thanks for talking plot and character development with me. And thanks to David, Brian, and Adam, for deciding that sometimes it's okay to read a book about a girl.

And finally, a big thank you to my readers! Thank you for spending a few hours with Tess on her journey. If her story helped you to see words a little differently, then I have more than succeeded.

Lauren Hallstrom is the author of the CIPA EVVY award-winning novel *Dreamweaver*, which she wrote at the age of 15 during National Novel Writing Month (NaNoWriMo), a nationwide challenge to write a novel in 30 days. Her novel won Douglas County Libraries' 2012 Teen NaNoWriMo contest and was chosen to be sponsored for publication. She won the contest for the second year in a row and published her second book, *One Hundred Words*, at the age of 17.

Lauren lives in Parker, Colorado with her parents, three younger brothers, and a hyper cat. When she's not homeschooling or working at the library, she spends her time reading voraciously, writing poetry, and, like Tess, always searching for the perfect words. Visit her online at www.laurenhallstrom.com.